D0068110

Dear Aldo —
It's almost Thanksgiving!
I'm thankful for you,
my little sketch
journalist.
What will you
give thanks for?
Fondly,
Goosy

ALDO,

Thirty days hath
November, April, June,
and September.
All the rest have thirty-one,
excepting February alone.
Begin.

— Mr. Mot

WHO'S WHO

ME – ALDO ZELNICK.

MY FINICKY BEST FRIEND, JACK.

MR. FODDER, MY SCHOOL'S LUNCH LADY WHO'S A GUY.

MY OTHER FRIENDS, DANNY (WHO'S DEAF) AND BEE (WHO'S ANNOYING).

FREEDOM

MR. MOT, NEIGHBOR, WORD GUY, AND FORMER ACTIVIST.

MRS. POOKER, SCHOOL LUNCH RUINER.

4

Finicky

AN ALDO ZELNICK COMIC NOVEL

Written by Karla Oceanak

Illustrated by Kendra Spanjer

BAILIWICK PRESS

DELETE

FAIRFAX PUBLIC LIBRARY
313 Vanderbilt Street
Fairfax, IA 52228
319-846-2994

FX:4-2

This is a work of fiction. Names, characters, places, and incidents are either the product of the author's imagination or are used fictitiously. Any resemblance to actual persons, living or dead, events, or locales is entirely coincidental.

First trade paperback edition 2016
Copyright © 2012, 2016 by Karla Oceanak and Kendra Spanjer

All rights reserved. No part of this publication may be reproduced, stored in a retrieval system, or transmitted in any form or by any means, electronic, mechanical, photocopying, or otherwise, without the prior written permission of the publisher.

Published by:
Bailiwick Press
309 East Mulberry Street
Fort Collins, Colorado 80524
(970) 672-4878
Fax: (970) 672-4731
www.bailiwickpress.com
www.aldozelnick.com

Book design by:
Launie Parry
Red Letter Creative
www.red-letter-creative.com

ISBN 978-1-934649-70-1

Library of Congress Control Number: 2016931915

MY FAMILY. MOM, DAD, AND MY SUPER-FIT BROTHER, TIMOTHY.

MY GRANDMA, GOOSY. FRUG-STER.

ABUELO AND MRS. LOPEZ.

JACK'S DAD, FRITZ.

BACON BOY, MY FOOD HERO... STAR OF MY VERY OWN COMICS.

BEE'S FAMILY AND SLOW FOODIES, THE GOODES: MR. GOODE, MRS. GOODE, AND VIVI.

5

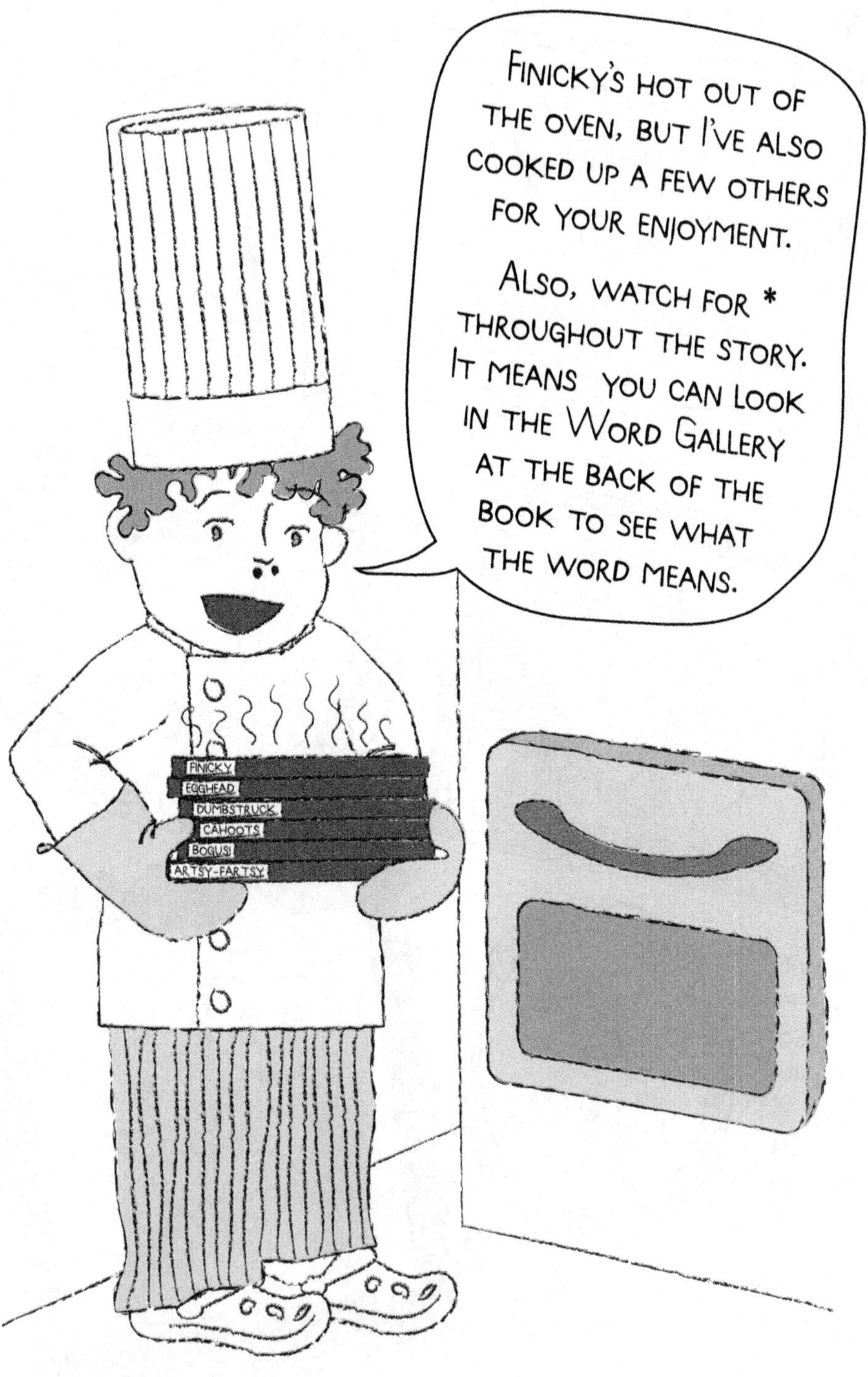
FINICKY'S HOT OUT OF THE OVEN, BUT I'VE ALSO COOKED UP A FEW OTHERS FOR YOUR ENJOYMENT.
ALSO, WATCH FOR * THROUGHOUT THE STORY. IT MEANS YOU CAN LOOK IN THE WORD GALLERY AT THE BACK OF THE BOOK TO SEE WHAT THE WORD MEANS.
FINICKY
EGGHEAD
DUMBSTRUCK
CAHOOTS
BOGUS!
ARTSY-FARTSY

PIZZA FAMINE*?

Ahhh. There's nothing like a slice of sausage pizza to put a big greasy smile on your face and a warm lump of bliss in your belly.

Today's Monday, so it was pizza lunch at Dana Elementary. The cafeteria serves pizza <u>every</u> Monday, which means on Sunday nights you have something to look forward to even though your weekend is, sadly, ancient history.

Even Jack likes pizza! I mean, there aren't many foods in this universe that my best friend will eat, but cheese pizza is one of them. He's so finicky* that he pretty much lives on peanut-butter sandwiches, plain bagels, noodles with butter, and cheese pizza. Our friend Bee says he's a beige-atarian.

So Jack and I were sitting there in the cafeteria enjoying Monday pizza. Bee was eating a salad she'd brought from home—green and red and orange and yellow all mixed together in a plastic bowl. It looked more like a Crayola shrub than a food, if you ask me.

That's when Mr. Fodder—he's a lunch lady who's a guy—walked up to us with a funny look on his face. He glanced both ways then leaned in close to whisper to me. His hairnetted beard was practically touching my cheek.

"Whaaa?" I choked. I can never tell whether Mr. Fodder is kidding or serious, but he had me seriously worried. "We have pizza every Monday!"

"There's talk of a new school menu," he shrugged. "Food that's 'healthier.'" He air-quoted around the word "healthier."

WHEN YOU "DRAW" QUOTATION MARKS IN THE AIR WITH YOUR FINGERS, IT MEANS YOU DON'T AGREE WITH THE WORDS YOU'RE PUTTING THE QUOTES AROUND. WEIRD.
(ALSO, JUST SO YOU KNOW, MR. FODDER THE LUNCH MAN IS NOT AS CRAZY OR AS CREEPY AS HE LOOKS.)

"But cheese pizza is one of my 4 food groups," mumbled Jack.

"Sorry, kid," said Mr. Fodder. "Hate to be the bearer of nauseating news." And he and his beard wobbled away.

Jack and I turned to glare at Bee and her veggie-lovers' salad.

"What?" she said. "I didn't have anything to do with this! Although I just <u>know</u> you will adore vegetables once you get used to them. Oh! I hope they put fennel on the menu! Fennel rocks."

I looked down at my last bite of pizza. I'd saved one flawless* pearl of sausage atop one perfect pillow of tomato-sauce-dotted crust. It glistened in the fluorescent* light shining down from the cafeteria ceiling. I placed it on my tongue, closed my eyes, and chewed.

Somehow it wasn't as awesome as always, which is what can happen with some of your favorite things when you make the mistake of examining them too closely.

A FEW OF MY FAVORITE THINGS

Sausage on pizza and 9-layer Slushies.
   Doughnuts, taquitos, and pies that aren't mushy.
Thanksgiving turkey and fried onion strings.
   These are a few of my favorite things...

Bacon on everything, kit and caboodle.
   Deviled eggs, Dagwoods, and cheesy-warm noodles.
Nachos with queso and buffalo wings.
   These are a few of my favorite things!

When my school stinks...
When my mood swings...
When I'm feeling sa-a-a-d...
I simply remember my favorite things
And then I don't fe-e-e-l so-o-o ba-a-a-d!

MOVING DAY

After school today, I met up at the tree fort with Jack and Bee. But neither of them really seemed in a fort frame of mind.*

Then it started snowing.

"That's it," sighed Jack. "We're gonna have to close up our fort for the winter, Aldo."

"Nah, it's just flurries.* Besides, we need a kids-only place to chillax, right? It's where we do our best thinking!"

"We can go to my house," suggested Bee, whose lips were turning an eerie shade of blue.

"Do you have Fritos at your house?"

"No."

"I didn't think so."

By now you could see everyone's breath. And OK, I'd lost some feeling in my toes. That's when I remembered the spare bag of Fritos I'd stashed in my bedroom closet—my <u>colossal</u> bedroom closet—and how my mom had been bugging me to clean it out...

BINGO! (I'M SO CAREFUL ABOUT MY CARBON FOOTPRINT* THESE DAYS, EVEN MY GREAT-IDEA LIGHTBULB IS THIS SQUIGGLY FLUORESCENT KIND.)

"Eureka!" I cried. "My bedroom closet is a behemoth. I think it's even bigger than this fort. We'll just move our fort to my <u>closet</u> for the winter!"

"B-b-b-bueno," shivered Jack. "¡Vamos!"

"If your parents give us permission...," said Bee with eyebrows raised for annoying emphasis, "it sounds perfect."

So we grabbed our fort furnishings* and hurried down the street to my casa. As soon as we pulled open the front door, an irresistible fragrance* lured us straight into the kitchen. There was my dad, frying up a batch of his famous fit-for-a-king* French fries, sprinkled with Parmesan cheese and chopped parsley.

"You kids look like you could use some hot food," he said. "Pull up a stool!"

"Thank you, Mr. Zelnick!" gushed Bee. "We were freezing. And these are the best fries I've ever tasted!"

"Could I have some <u>without</u> the white and green stuff, Mr. Z?" asked Jack, and Dad passed him his own plate of fries with plain salt.

"Would you share this recipe with my parents?" asked Bee. "Maybe they'll put it on the menu at our restaurant!"

With my mouth full of ketchup and fries, I asked Bee, "Zhew myav ha nyestuyan?"

LOVELY, ALDO. I DON'T SPEAK "HOG", YOU KNOW!

Her expression told me she didn't comprehend, so I swallowed, burped, and tried again. "You have a restaurant? How come I didn't I know about this?"

"Because it's just getting started, silly. My parents and some friends are opening a restaurant called Fare.* It's going to have vegetarian dishes and other things that are organic and yummy."

"So you're saying it's a vegetable restaurant," I summarized.

"Not really. There will also be locally raised meat, amazing pizza, and lots of other choices."

"Can we please stop talking about food?" moaned Jack. Sometimes he gets as grossed out about food words as he does about actual food.

"Well, the Zelnicks want to be standing in line when your restaurant doors open!" exclaimed Dad. "When can we make reservations?"

"Right after Thanksgiving," said Bee.

"I'm fired up* to try it," said Dad. "Aren't you fired up, Aldo?"

"Um, maybe, but I'll tell you what I <u>am</u> fired up about," I said, changing the subject. "We're moving our fort into my closet for the winter."

"If it's OK with you and Mrs. Zelnick," added Bee.

"Fine by me!" said Dad. Then, leaning over to whisper in my ear, he added, "Have they ever <u>seen</u> the inside of your closet, sport?"

"They're about to," I whispered back.

So with full, warm bellies and festive* spirits, Jack and Bee followed me upstairs to feast their eyes on our new winter quarters...

F.E.A.S.T.

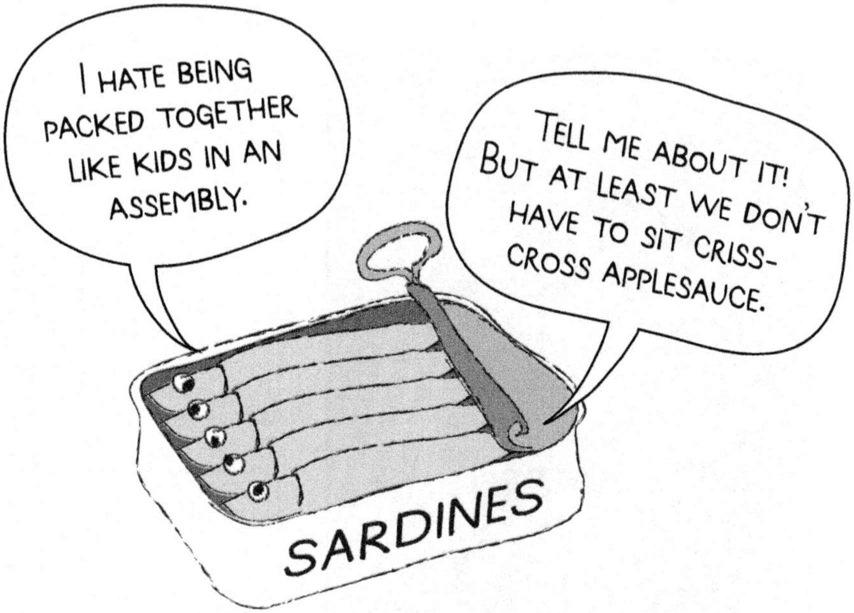
I HATE BEING PACKED TOGETHER LIKE KIDS IN AN ASSEMBLY.
TELL ME ABOUT IT! BUT AT LEAST WE DON'T HAVE TO SIT CRISS-CROSS APPLESAUCE.
SARDINES

Today we had an appalling school assembly.

Now, normally I love assemblies, because you do nothing but sit there and be entertained, which I'm good at. But my pants were a little snug (my mom must have shrunk them again), which made sitting on the hard floor extra-excruciating. And today's assembly was about the new cafeteria food Mr. Fodder warned us about.

"We're here today to celebrate our health!" boomed Principal Dobrowski into the microphone once all of us kids were packed on the gym floor like sardines who can sit up. "Out of all the elementary schools here in our fantastic* town of Fort Collins, Dana Elementary has the privilege of being the <u>one and only</u> school chosen to test the school district's new cafeteria menu. The program is called F.E.A.S.T, and it stands for Food Energy And Sensational Tastes."

Mr. Dobrowski did that thing where you pause because you expect the audience to clap. But nobody did, so he stumbled on.

...ANYONE?

"So...without further ado,* here's the school district's nutritionist, Mrs. Pooker, to tell you more about F.E.A.S.T.!"

A lady in a fish costume minced onto the stage.

"In the coming weeks," she proclaimed, "you'll be tasting interesting new flavors and enjoying foods that will provide you with better nutrition and more energy, so your bodies and brains will be prepared to learn!"

("My body and brain are going into shock," I whispered to Jack.)

"I'm dressed like this today," continued Mrs. Pooker, "because fish is a food that's especially good for your bodies and brains. In fact, it's so good that we'll be serving it every Friday!"

("Whew...at least she didn't say Monday," whispered Jack.)

"And there are lots more delicious surprises in store!" she added before floundering* away from the microphone.

("Ack...," I strangled. I pulled a lint-covered Atomic Fireball* from my pocket and furtively* slid it into my mouth. When I'm nervous, I nibble.)

"OK boys and girls, let's give Mrs. Pooker a big Dingo thank you!" said Mr. Dobrowski.

At Dana Elementary, our school mascot is the dingo, and when our principal says "a big Dingo thank you," he means we're all supposed to howl. Getting to howl as loud as

WOOOOOOO!

you can in school—especially in a gymful of other howling kids—is pretty cool, I must admit, and I have always loved working up a good Dingo howl.

But this was the first assembly of 5th grade, and as my classmates and I looked around at each other, we suddenly realized that 5th graders don't howl, they roll their eyes.

So yup. Today life tried to take away in-school howling and, if Mr. Fodder is right, pizza, all in one fell swoop.* But let me tell you something, Mrs. Pooker: Aldo Zelnick doesn't give up that easily. Nothing comes between me and my pizza, except sometimes an ice-cold carton of chocolate milk.

STUDIES SHOW THAT CHOCOLATE MILK IS 1 MILLION PERCENT TASTIER THAN REGULAR MILK. DON'T YOU AGREE?

BACON BOY IN ALL THIS FOOD TALK IS MAKING ME HUNGRY

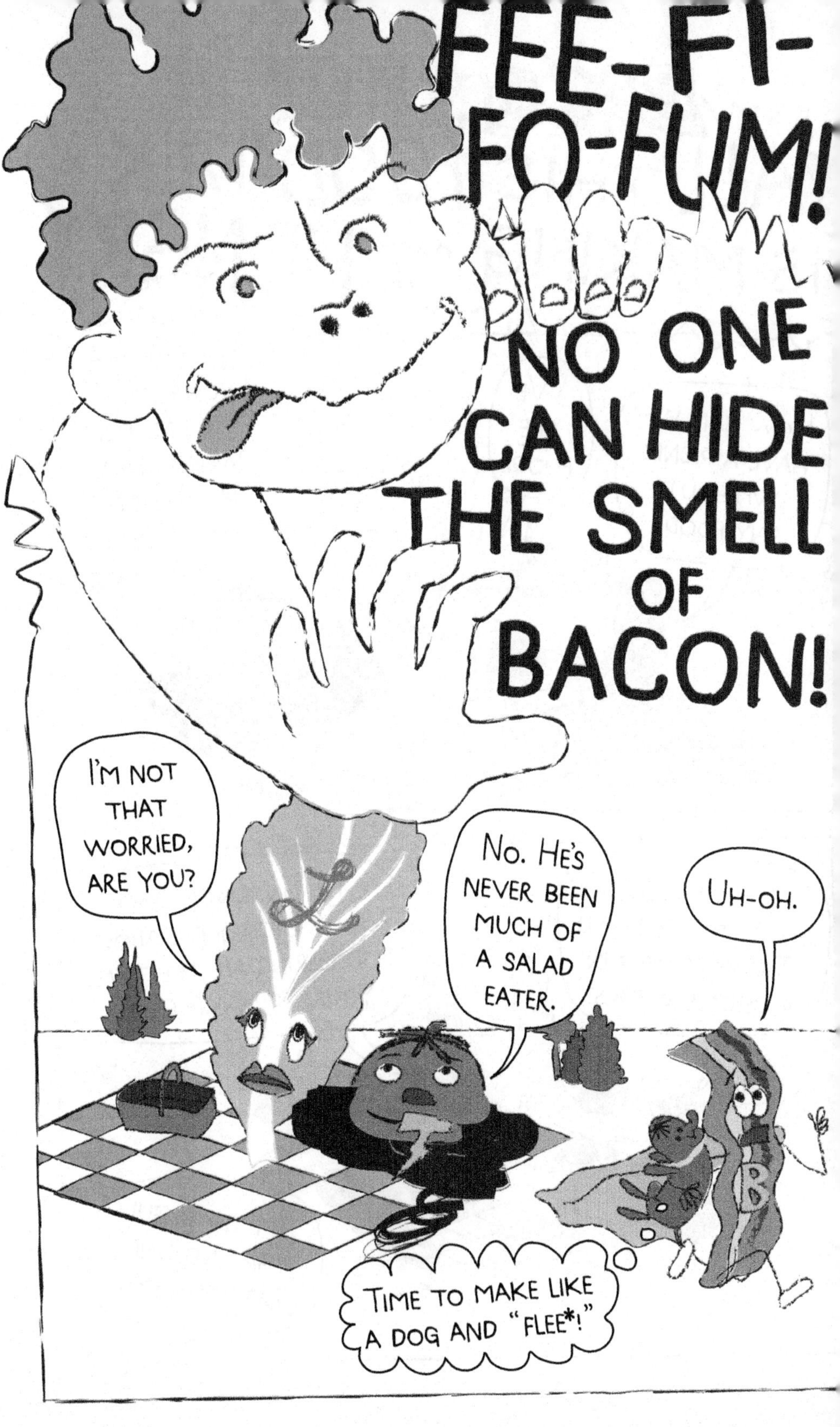
FEE-FI-FO-FUM!
NO ONE CAN HIDE THE SMELL OF BACON!
I'M NOT THAT WORRIED, ARE YOU?
NO. HE'S NEVER BEEN MUCH OF A SALAD EATER.
UH-OH.
TIME TO MAKE LIKE A DOG AND "FLEE*!"

FINE-FEATHERED FRIEND*

5TH GRADERS DON'T NEED MOMS AT SCHOOL ANYMORE, MOM.

BUT WHO'S GOING TO TELL YOU TO WASH YOUR HANDS AND TUCK IN YOUR SHIRT?

My mom came to my classroom today. Sheesh. When I was little, I sorta liked it when she volunteered at my school. For example, when I was in kindergarten, she was the shoe-tying lady on Fridays. I think she was <u>supposed</u> to be there helping us learn to draw our letters or count to 5 or something. But instead, all the kids would go to her when their laces were dragging, which was every 5 seconds.

(Me, I always wear slip-ons, so to this day I barely know how to tie shoelaces. But that can be our little secret.)

Since I'm in 5th now, I told Mom she shouldn't hang out at my school anymore...and she hasn't—until today. But I guess this one time it was cool, because she didn't just bring her own self, she also brought a big bird in a cage.

"I absolutely love birds," Mom told the class, "so one of the things I do with my free time is hang out with Aldo, because he's such a turkey. Just kidding, honey. Actually, I help out at the raptor center, which is like a hospital for birds of prey who've been injured. Who can tell me what a bird of prey is?"

I was still reeling from being called "honey" in public by my mom when Fiona raised her hand. "The main one I can think of is that white bird in the stained-glass window at my church."

"I'm guessing that's a dove," said Mom. "So you must be thinking of pray with an 'A-Y.' This is the 'E-Y' kind. Does anyone else have an idea?"

Farrukh raised his hand. "Birds of prey hunt other animals and eat them."

"That's right. Birds of prey—which are also called raptors—are predators. Like tigers and wolves and sharks, they hunt for their suppers. They're carnivores, which means they eat only meat."

"And fur and bones and eyeballs and stuff,"
I added as I furtively licked some Fun Dip powder
from my fingers. It must have spilled inside my desk
at our school Halloween party last month.

"Yes, Aldo. They eat most of their prey's
body parts because that's what their bodies need
for complete nutrition. If raptors went to the
butcher like we do, they'd ask for their meat
untrimmed."

"We take care of all species of birds of prey at the raptor center," Mom added, "like eagles, osprey, owls, and hawks. But today I brought with me..." and, wearing big leather gloves, she carefully lifted a real live bird out of the cage.

"Ooohhh...," the class said.

"...this lovely peregrine falcon. She was brought to the center a few years ago with a badly broken wing. And even though her injury healed, her wing will never be strong enough for her to survive in the wild. So the raptor center is her home now. We call her and the other birds who can't be released our "educational ambassadors," and we take them out into the community to teach you about raptors. Isn't she something?"

"What does she eat?" asked Marvin.

"At the center, we feed the injured falcons pieces of quail and duck. In the wild, where they have to fend* for themselves, peregrine falcons hunt other birds...maybe even that dove Fiona mentioned."

"Ew," said Fiona.

While the rest of the kids asked a bazillion more questions, I watched the falcon. She just sat there and blinked at us, turning her head from side-to-side like she was listening to what everyone said about her. Her feet and toes were bright yellow, with three toes and a thumb on each foot. On the end of each toe was a black, uber-sharp, curved claw.

I bet she'd rip you to shreds if you tried to take away her sausage pizza. Well, her dove.

LET'S SWAP. DOVE FOR YOU; PIZZA FOR ME.

NUMERICALLY CHALLENGED

EVERYBODY KEEPS SAYING I'M AN 8-POUNDER. WHAT IS THIS, A FISHING TOURNAMENT?

FRESHWATER ZELNICK

THIS BOOK SEEMS PRETTY FISHY AND IT'S ONLY PAGE 37.

CATCH O' THE DAY

Why do we have to put numbers on everybody?

When you're born, it's all about your inches and pounds. When you go to school, everybody wants to know your age. Your grade. Your test scores. Your reading level. Your sit-ups-in-a-minute count.

Sigh.

We started our fitness testing unit in P.E. today. It's the worst unit of the year in the worst class of life. I mean, how many times does my gym teacher have to see me <u>not</u> be able to do a pull-up to know that I <u>can't</u> do a pull-up?

"Every year for Presidential Fitness Testing we measure how many pull-ups and sit-ups you can do in a minute, how fast you can run, and other things to make sure you're physically fit," Mrs. Dalloway, our gym teacher, reminded us. (Like I needed reminding.)

"But this year we've decided to add a couple other important measurements of your health. We're going to record your weight and your height so we can calculate your Body Mass Index, or BMI. I'll be sending a note home to your parents with your BMI score and an explanation of what it means."

Then one by one, in the middle of sit-up testing (sweet! a break!), Mrs. Dalloway sent us to the nurse's office. My brother calls me "Chub" sometimes, and my mom's constantly telling me I need to get more exercise...and I know I'm a little short for my weight, so I figured this wouldn't be good. But Nurse Dolores weighed me and checked my height like it was no big deal!

Welp, then after school, Jack and I walked home together, like we do every day.

"Wanna sleep over at my dad-house this weekend?" he asked.

"Sure," I shrugged. (Jack has a dad-house and a mom-house. His parents are divorced, but they live just down the street from each other.) "Hey, I've got some couch money in my backpack," I remembered. (Couch money is the random coins you find in places like underneath your couch cushions and on your brother's bedroom floor.) "Wanna go get doughnuts and taquitos?"

Sure," he shrugged back, and we set off toward the convenience store. "Yeah, I probably <u>do</u> need to eat more," he added. "Nurse Dolores said I'm only a 14."

"You are? What are you supposed to be?"

"Like an 18, I think."

"What am <u>I</u> supposed to be?"

"Like an 18."

"But you're taller than me! And isn't it out of 100?"

"No. I think it's out of 25 or something."

I thought about that for a few seconds. Maybe 22 isn't such a nice, happy number after all, according to their dumb numbering system. So when we got to the convenience store, I had to decide whether to cut a doughnut or a taquito out of my usual order. Sheesh.

HEY DOUGHBOY! ROCK, PAPER, SCISSORS?

YOU'RE GOING DOWN! DOWN WITH A LARGE SLUSHIE, THAT IS.

F.E.A.S.T.? MY FOOT*!

Fancy new posters with loads of exclamation marks have started popping up around school, filling me with a sense of foreboding.*

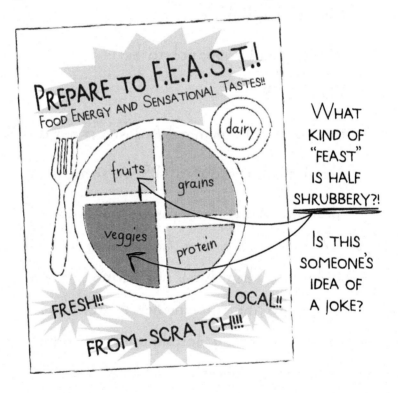

PREPARE TO F.E.A.S.T.!
FOOD ENERGY AND SENSATIONAL TASTES!!

dairy

fruits

grains

veggies

protein

FRESH!!

LOCAL!!

FROM-SCRATCH!!!

WHAT KIND OF "FEAST" IS HALF SHRUBBERY?!

IS THIS SOMEONE'S IDEA OF A JOKE?

I stopped to read one of the posters today in the cafeteria right after lunch, which was the delicious duo of crispy chicken sandwich and tater tots. I was just chewing my last tot as Mr. Fodder walked by. He was holding a measuring tape.

"When is this F.E.A.S.T. thing starting exactly?" I asked him.

"Next week. Here's where the new salad bar's going," he added, drawing imaginary lines with his hands to help me picture this carrot cart.

My stomach rumbled with apprehension.

"SALAD BAR" IS CODE FOR "RABBIT FOOD"—AS FAR AS THE EYE CAN SEE, ZELNICK. AS FAR AS THE EYE CAN SEE...

IT'S ON WHEELS? WILL IT FOLLOW ME AROUND?

"What else is changing?"

"Chocolate milk—annihilated." He drew the pointer finger of his left hand across his throat as he said it.

"No!"

WCHHKT!

"Yessiree-bob."

"Why??! It's milk!"

"Too much 'sugar,'" he said. "Too many 'calories.'" His netted beard bounced up and down whenever he air-quoted.

"Gah! I think calories are fictitious.* Like unicorns. I mean, nobody's ever seen them!"

BLUB!

BLUB!

BLUB!

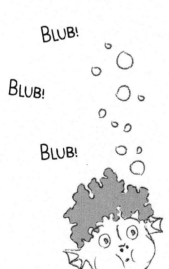

"You won't be able to see chocolate milk anymore either, pal."

And he walked away, leaving me to flounder in my disbelief.

ALDO'S ARMY

When something you care deeply about is under attack, you have to take a stand. It's your duty as a citizen and a human being, right?

By the time I got home from school, I'd gone from denial and disbelief about the cafeteria changes to fury.* So I called a fort meeting to talk about fighting back against F.E.A.S.T. I invited Danny, too, since an army needs more than 3 people.

(By the way, the new closet fort is pretty sweet. We worked hard to get everything straightened up and fort-worthy. It's not quite as private as our outdoor fort, but we made a sign for the door to discourage uninvited guests, Timothy.)

PRIVATE PROPERTY!

KEEP OUT!!!

Intruders will be prosecuted to the full extent of the law.

(THIS MEANS YOU, TIMOTHY.)

Top-secret meeting ❋ in progress. ❋ DO NOT ENTER! (UNLESS YOU'RE BRINGING SNACKS)

I sat in the bean-bag chair of leadership and called the meeting to order.

"It's looking like F.E.A.S.T. is anything but," I began. Since I was feeling pretty feebish* by now, I munched on some ancient Funyuns I'd unearthed during closet clean-up.

"We can't let Mrs. Pooker and her gang bully us like this!" I campaigned, picking up steam. "Today they're taking away chocolate milk. What'll it be tomorrow? Water? Are they gonna lock up the drinking fountains and throw away the key? We _have_ to do something about this."

"You're being absurd," said Bee. "The salad bar's going to be fabulous*!"

"If by fabulous you mean disgusting... Hey, whose side are you on, anyway?"

"I bring peanut-butter sandwiches a lot anyway," said Jack. "I'll just eat _them_ every day."

"That's not a very balanced diet, Jack—not without cheese pizza. Besides, they can't just wipe an entire food group off the face of the menu!"

"Yeah. I guess you're right."

"How 'bout you, Danny? What's your favorite school lunch?"

"Chicken nuggets," he wrote on a piece of paper. (Danny's deaf, so he talks with his hands— in sign language and writing.)

"Well I don't know for sure if chicken nuggets are in danger of flying the coop,* but I'm guessing they might be."

WHAT PART OF THE CHICKEN IS THE NUGGET EXACTLY?

ALL THE MOST DELICIOUS PARTS SMOOSHED TOGETHER.

"Aldo, Mr. Dobrowski said they're <u>testing</u> the F.E.A.S.T. program at Dana Elementary," pointed out Bee. "That means they'll listen to us. They don't want to serve lunches that kids won't eat. That wouldn't make any sense!"

IF YOU'RE ANGRY AND YOU KNOW IT, FROWN A FROWN.

"Anyway. Here's what I propose," I said. "Let's start a petition to keep pizza, chicken nuggets, and chocolate milk on the menu. And we'll make posters to put around the school too. Everywhere there's a F.E.A.S.T. poster, we'll put one of ours next to it."

"I do like making posters...," said Bee.

"We're gonna need a slogan," I said. "Every good campaign has a slogan."

Danny held up a little scrap of paper:

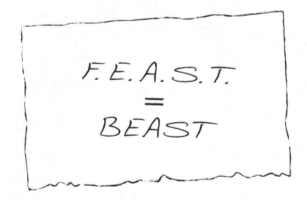

F. E. A. S. T.
=
BEAST

"F.E.A.S.T. is a BEAST! Perfect. Let's do it."

So we spent a couple hours making posters to hang up at school tomorrow. I have a feeling that Mr. Fodder's gonna like them.

F.E.A.S.T. IS A BEAST!

DID YOU KNOW?

School pizza is in danger of becoming EXTINCT under the new cafeteria program!

See Aldo Zelnick to sign the petition to keep pizza on the menu.

F.E.A.S.T. is a BEAST
Take it from me: I'm a fat beast, and even I can't stomach that stuff.
PLEASE SIGN DANNY PETERSON'S PETITION
Chicken nuggets: For Here! Not To-Go!

F.E.A.S.T.
is a
Beast.

Um, I don't like to talk about food, so...
All I ask is that you keep cheese pizza.

Por favor y Gracias.

beast

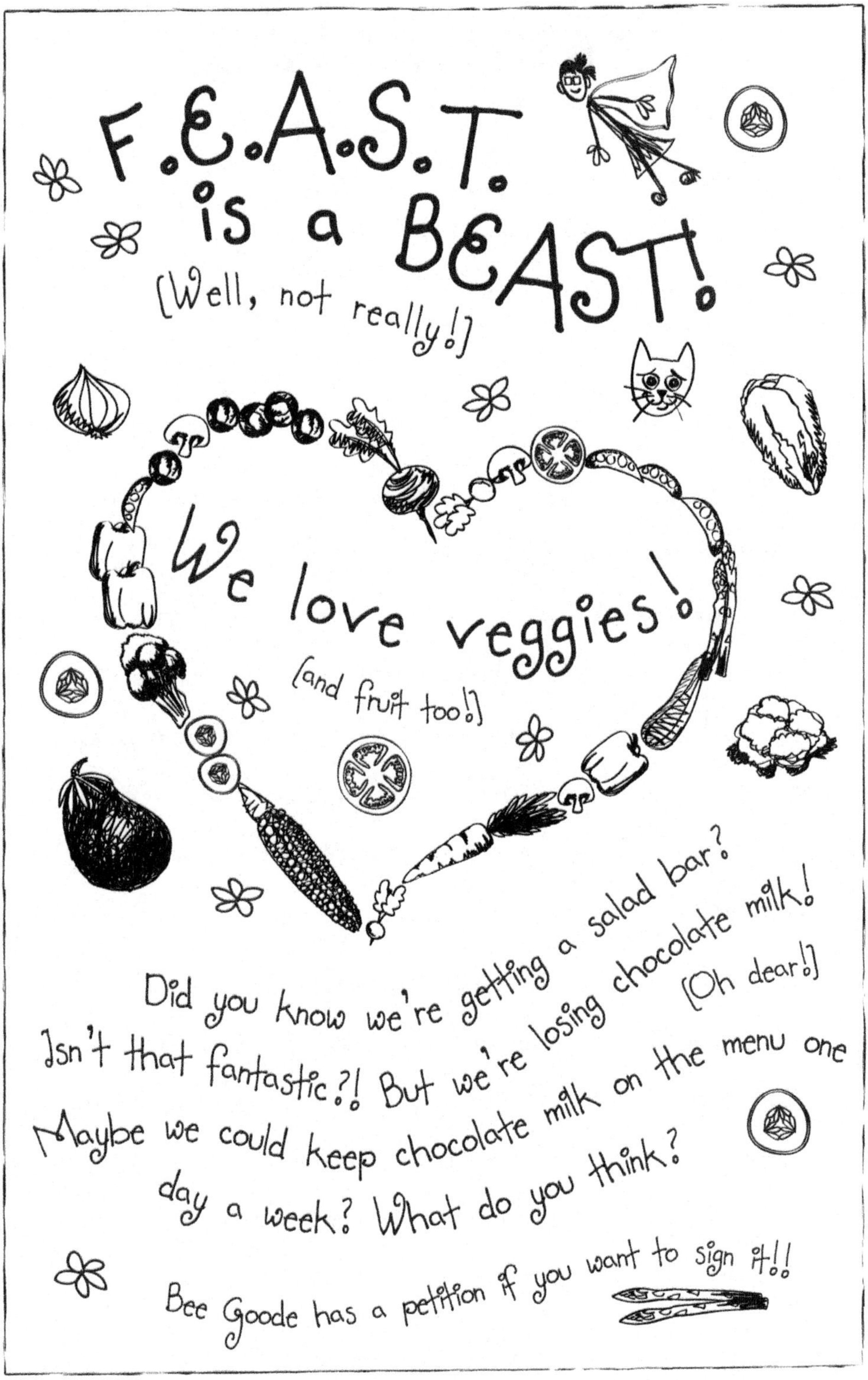
F.E.A.S.T. is a BEAST!
[Well, not really!]
We love veggies!
[and fruit too!]
Did you know we're getting a salad bar? Isn't that fantastic?! But we're losing chocolate milk! [Oh dear!] Maybe we could keep chocolate milk on the menu one day a week? What do you think?
Bee Goode has a petition if you want to sign it!!

ARCIMBOLDO

Today in Art, Ms. Munroe taught us about this fantastic artist from a long time ago. He lived during the 1500s—way before electricity or TV or fast food. (Although he <u>was</u> Italian, so maybe he at least got to have pizza. I mean geez, what if I had been born before pizza was invented? That would have been the tragedy of my life, and I wouldn't even have known it.)

"Since our school community is having such an important conversation about food right now," said Ms. Munroe, "I thought we should study one of history's most fascinating painters. His name was Giuseppe Arcimboldo, and he painted portraits of people...using food."

I was imagining someone trying to paint with a burrito or a broccoli stalk instead of a brush when Ms. Munroe showed us some slides of his paintings. I was way off! I can't even explain how cool they are. Basically, he painted really realistic vegetables and meat and flowers and fish and stuff, arranging them so the whole food-clump looks like a person when you see it from far away.

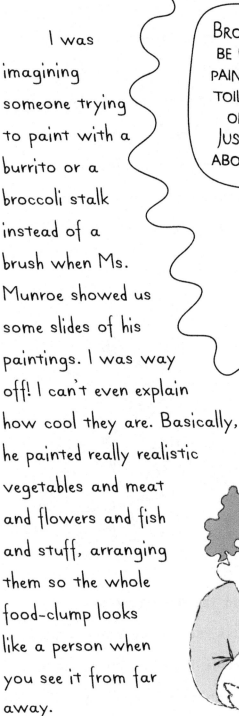

Then we got started on making our own self-portraits Arcimboldo-style. To get in the mood, I grabbed a Fig Newton* from my backpack and popped it into my mouth. Ms. Munroe said we could either <u>draw</u> the foods or cut out pictures of food from magazines. She showed us how to look for food shapes that kind of match up with shapes in our faces. Like this:

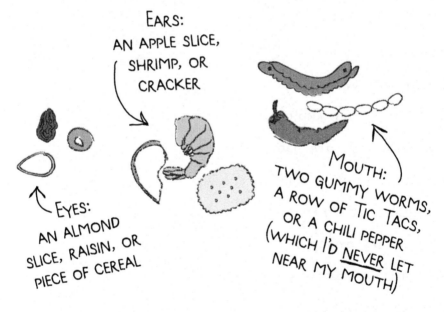

EARS:
AN APPLE SLICE, SHRIMP, OR CRACKER

EYES:
AN ALMOND SLICE, RAISIN, OR PIECE OF CEREAL

MOUTH:
TWO GUMMY WORMS, A ROW OF TIC TACS, OR A CHILI PEPPER (WHICH I'D <u>NEVER</u> LET NEAR MY MOUTH)

We're going to spend the next few art classes on our self-portraits, so I have some time to work on it. But I did decide that for mine, I'm going to try to use drawings of some of my <u>favorite</u> foods.

After I got home from school, I looked up Arcimboldo's portraits on Wikipaintings.org and printed out one called "Vertumnus." I taped it here so you can see what I'm talking about:

GRAPES

PEAR

PEACH

FUZZY FRUIT?

Weird, huh?

Is this what they mean when they say, "You are what you eat"?

Later in the day Danny and I got permission from Mr. Dobrowski to hang our "F.E.A.S.T. is a BEAST" posters around the school. They look pretty fierce* if I do say so myself. Now all we have to do is sit back and let the posters do the work of convincing Mrs. Pooker and everyone else that F.E.A.S.T. is totally for the birds.*

COMFORT FOOD

I brought home the parent letter about BMI and my 22 score today. Mom and Dad and Timothy were in the kitchen. Mom was paying bills, Dad was getting dinner started, and Timothy was showing off, as per usual. I opened a bag of fudge-striped cookies and handed Mom the note.

"Oh look...they measured Aldo's body mass index at school!" she said. "That's a good idea, isn't it, Leo? We all need to be more aware of managing our weight."

"Yes, I suppose so," sighed Leo/Dad.

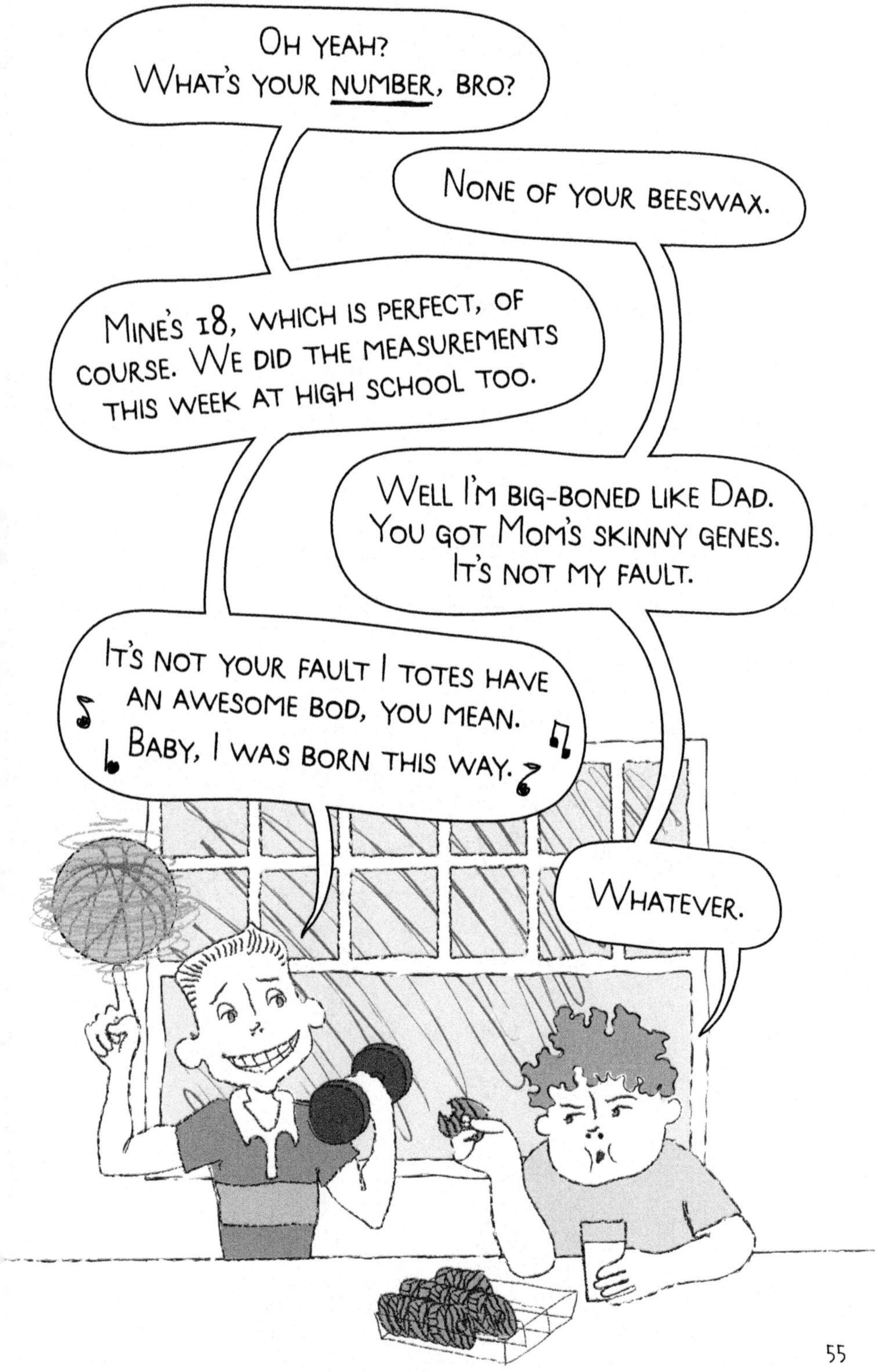
OH YEAH? WHAT'S YOUR NUMBER, BRO?
NONE OF YOUR BEESWAX.
MINE'S 18, WHICH IS PERFECT, OF COURSE. WE DID THE MEASUREMENTS THIS WEEK AT HIGH SCHOOL TOO.
WELL I'M BIG-BONED LIKE DAD. YOU GOT MOM'S SKINNY GENES. IT'S NOT MY FAULT.
IT'S NOT YOUR FAULT I TOTES HAVE AN AWESOME BOD, YOU MEAN. BABY, I WAS BORN THIS WAY.
WHATEVER.

"Aldo, your number is pretty high," said Mom. "We need to get you more active. Is there any winter sport you could do?"

"News flash: I hate sports!"

"Well, maybe you can help me at the raptor center. Let's think on it and talk about it later tonight. Right now Timothy and I are on our way to the store to get new running shoes!"

And with that, Mom and Timothy ran off, leaving Dad and me alone with our potbellies in the floury kitchen dust.

MY PANTS ARE TOO SMALL. MOM MUST BE SHRINKING THEM IN THE DRYER.

SHE MUST BE SHRINKING MINE TOO, SPORT. EITHER THAT OR I'M HAVING TWINS.

"My doctor said I need to bring down my BMI too, Aldo," said Dad. "The list of health problems caused by being overweight starts to get pretty serious at my age."

"But you're not that fat!"

"You flatter* me. According to Dr. Ferrell, I've got a good 30 pounds to lose. And my dad had heart problems, remember?"

"Pffft. You're fine."

"How about we try to help each other?"

"Like how?"

"Like, let's go shoot baskets in the driveway. We can play FOX." FOX is what we play when we're feeling too lazy to play HORSE.

"OK," I said. "But I get to go first."

"Deal."

So Dad and I played 5 games of FOX. Mom and Timothy joined us when they got back home. I have to admit it was medium fun. Timothy even let me win—one whole letter.

FREAKY*
FRIDAY

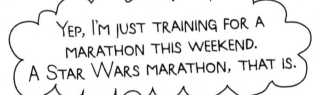

It's Friday, which is pretty much the best day ever invented. I mean, it's the last day of school for the week, so you have the whole weekend ahead of you. All the teachers are a little more relaxed. Mr. Krug even lets us play a math game during math class on Friday mornings.

So I didn't let it get me down when we had to do the shuttle-run fitness test in P.E. today.

The shuttle run is this crazy race where you pick up a bean bag and run with it till you get to a certain line, then you set it down quickly, pick up another bag, run to another line. You go back and forth like that as fast as you can, stopping and starting and beanbag-putting-down-and-grabbing. And all the while someone's timing you with a stopwatch. It's asinine! And yeah, I got the worst time in my class on the shuttle run.

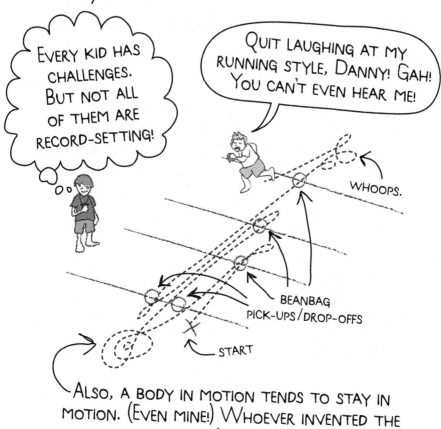

EVERY KID HAS CHALLENGES. BUT NOT ALL OF THEM ARE RECORD-SETTING!

QUIT LAUGHING AT MY RUNNING STYLE, DANNY! GAH! YOU CAN'T EVEN HEAR ME!

WHOOPS.

BEANBAG PICK-UPS/DROP-OFFS

START

ALSO, A BODY IN MOTION TENDS TO STAY IN MOTION. (EVEN MINE!) WHOEVER INVENTED THE SHUTTLE RUN MUST'VE FAILED PHYSICS TOO.

Then even after I saw what was for lunch, I still kept trying to stay in a Friday frame of mind. On Fridays we used to have fish sticks with tartar sauce and French fries once in a while, but today, thanks to F.E.A.S.T., we had baked fish covered in little brown bug-like flax seeds (whatever they are) and some weirdo salad called fattoush.* I ate a couple bites, but I noticed most kids picking at theirs then throwing it away. By the time I went to after-lunch recess, the cafeteria's scrape-off-your-tray trash cans were overflowing.

I'm home from school now, and as I'm writing this, I'm starting to realize that 4 measly F.E.A.S.T. is a BEAST posters might not be enough to fix this menu mess after all...

OK. I just called Bee and Jack and Danny. Danny's busy, but Jack and I are going to Bee's house to figure out what to do next. B4N.

As it turned out, my Friday only got freakier after that.

The first thing Bee did when we got to her house was show us her fungus* factory, which she keeps on a table in her bedroom. Seriously, the girl's got a dish filled with a brick of sawdust that she grows mushrooms on. For <u>eating</u>. Guh-ross.

There's a fungus among us!

("How can eating fungus possibly be good for you?!" I whispered to Jack.)

("Just <u>looking</u> at it's not good for me," he whispered back.)

Then we gathered around Bee's kitchen table to talk strategy.

"That school lunch today was NOT good," I said. "Fish sticks are a bazillion times better."

"I agree," said Bee.

"You do?"

"Of course! Food that's good for you doesn't have to taste dreadful. That fish was icky."

I'VE NEVER SEEN BEE MAKE THIS FACE ABOUT HEALTH FOOD! (IT WAS <u>THAT BAD.</u>)

"OK then! But I've been thinking, what if the posters alone don't do the trick? Then what?"

"We have to get lots of kids to sign our petitions. At least the fish fiasco* will help with that."

"Good. Anything else?"

"Back in my day we staged sit-ins," said a familiar voice from across the room. It was our neighbor friend, Mr. Mot! He was quietly fussing with food of some kind on the kitchen counter.

"What are you doing at Bee's house?" I asked, surprised. I hadn't noticed him till just then.

"I promised to demonstrate for the Goodes how I prepare my famous cracker-thin pizza crust. Perhaps they will care to follow my example in their restaurant."

"We just slid a pizza into the oven, kids," said Mr. Goode. "There's plenty for everyone."

"What's a sit-in?" asked Jack.

"A sit-in is a form of protest in which you and your fellow activists occupy a space that belongs to those in authority," said Mr. Mot, who's the only person I know who talks like that. "You simply remain quietly seated."

"You just sit there? Let's do that!" I said. "I'd totally be good at that."

"So you'll be sitting in to keep pizza on the school menu, is that right, Aldo?" asked Mrs. Goode.

"Yup. And chicken nuggets and chocolate milk."

"Sometimes those who are sitting-in lock their arms together in solidarity," added Mr. Mot. "Shall we rehearse?"

So us kids sat on the floor with Mr. Mot while Bee's parents kept making pizzas. He showed us how to hook our arms together at the elbows.

ALDO'S ALWAYS HAD A FLAIR* FOR SITTING.

I DO MISS A GOOD SIT-IN.

THIS REQUIRES EVEN LESS EFFORT THAN I EXPECTED!

Pretty soon I smelled pizza smell though. That got me up off the floor and back to the table, where Mr. Goode had just plopped down the weird-looking, pizza-like concoction he had been blathering about.

THE PROBLEM WITH TYPICAL PIZZA IS THAT IT DOESN'T GIVE YOU MUCH NUTRITION, CALORIE-FOR-CALORIE... BLAH BLAH BLAH BLAH BLAH...

...THIS LOVELY PIE, HOWEVER, BLAH BLAH **CARAMELIZED ONIONS**, ROASTED **SWEET POTATOES**, BLAH BLAH **TURKEY-HERB SAUSAGE** AND BLAH BLAH BLAH GOAT **CHEESE**. BLAH BLAH VITAMINS BLAH ANTIOXIDANTS AND BLAH BLAH BLAH BLAH BLAH...

"No thanks," said Jack. "I already ate once today. And can we maybe <u>not</u> use so many food words?" (That kid's never gonna get anywhere close to an 18 score if he keeps being that finicky.)

"Never say no to pizza, that's my motto!" I said, and I bit into a slice. It tasted kinda weird, kinda good. I noticed that the two Misters were waiting for my opinion.

"I'm normally a deep-dish kind of guy," I said to Mr. Mot, "but I <u>am</u> enjoying this crust." And the pizza itself? I took another bite and exaggeratedly dragged it around my taste buds. "It tastes like pizza and Thanksgiving dinner got smashed together in an accident," I pronounced.

While we feasted, Mr. Mot told us about other ways to protest, like picketing, marching, and chanting. Chanting's where you make up a catchy saying for your group to yell over and over again so your opinion is heard loud and clear. He said people who were against the Vietnam war used this one a lot:

STOP THE WAR! FEED THE POOR!

I think I'll work on an anti-F.E.A.S.T. chant this weekend in case we need one.

Oh, and then to round out this day of weirdness, we watched an old movie called *Freaky Friday*. It's about a mom and daughter who accidentally trade bodies, so the mom is living in the girl's body and vice versa. At least if I traded bodies with my dad, I could go buy whatever I wanted for lunch.

DID SOMEONE SAY "DRIVE-THRU"?

SO I THINK
I CAN'T DANCE

Ah, Saturday morning.

If Friday is the best overall day of the week, Saturday's gotta be the best <u>morning</u> of the week. And the best Saturday mornings of all are the ones where you don't have anything to do...so you sleep as late as you want, get up and eat some bacon and an apple fritter* or whatever yumminess your dad's made, play computer games, then pretty much veg out until dinnertime.

But today when I ambled downstairs, basking in that glowy, do-nothing feeling, Goosy was waiting for me in the kitchen. She brings a lot of energy to any situation. And her high energy was making my laziness apprehensive.

"Good morning, sleepyhead!" she said. "I've been waiting for you! We have dance class in half an hour!"

ME, THE GROOVE, AND MY FRIENDS ARE GONNA TRY TO MOVE YOUR FEET!

"Who's 'we'?" I frowned.

"You and I! I signed us up for a disco class on Saturday mornings. We're gonna boogie together. Don't be a fuddy-duddy*!"

"Um, no thanks."

"Aldo, remember how we talked about you needing more physical activity?" said Mom. "Remember that <u>number</u> we discussed?"

"I'm Not. Going. To a Dance Class."

"OK, well, it's getting to be winter, so I guess that means basketball then. I'll get you on the basketball team at school."

Basketball = constant running = worse than dancing (if that's even possible).

"We promised to help each other, Aldo," said Dad, "so how about if I go to dance class too?"

I looked at the circle of enthusiastic faces looking at me, from Goosy to Mom to Dad, as I bit into a bagel. "Aw geez. I'm going to dance class, aren't I."

"Let's hustle!" cried Goosy.

And that's how it happened that I spent my fleetingly* lazy Saturday morning learning how to dance "The Frug*" with my dad and my grandma.

TRUMAN CAPOTE TAUGHT ME THE FRUG AT THE ARTHUR CLUB.

GOOSY TAUGHT ME THE FRUG IN OUR FRONT YARD WHEN I WAS JUST A LITTLE FELLOW.

SIGH. I GUESS I WAS FATED* TO FRUG.

THE MAN OF FEW FOODS
(AND EVEN FEWER WORDS)

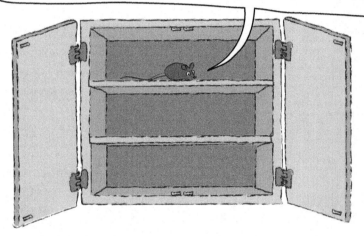

C'MON BUDDY. I'M BELOW YOU ON THE FOOD CHAIN,* SO IF YOU'RE NOT GOING TO KEEP ANY FOOD IN HERE, THE LEAST YOU COULD DO IS NOT BE QUITE SO FASTIDIOUS.*

The first thing you need to know about Jack's dad-house is that it's a food-free zone.

I mean sure, there's bread and peanut butter and milk and yogurt, but there are no actual <u>meals</u>, like the roast-beef-mashed-potato-and-broccoli-with-cheese-sauce dinner we had at my house last Sunday. I think Jack and his dad mostly use the kitchen for sandwich-making, snack-eating, and homework-doing.

JACK'S DAD IS A FIREMAN. HE EXERCISES TO STAY IN SHAPE. IT'S LIKE HIS BODY IS A MACHINE HE USES TO DO HIS WORK, SO HE HAS TO KEEP IT FAST AND LEAN. JACK'S BUILT JUST LIKE HIM. FASCINATING. MY BODY IS MORE LIKE AN ENJOYMENT DEVICE THAT I USE TO DO FUN THINGS THAT DON'T INVOLVE MOVING AROUND, INCLUDING EATING. JACK'S DOG, SLATE—HIS BODY IS MORE OR LESS A FLATULENCE* CONTRAPTION.

Jack's mom is a foodie* like me, but Jack and his dad, they're survival eaters. They eat to live instead of the other way around. So while I'm constantly trying to finagle* invitations to a meal at Jack's mom-house, I usually try to avoid ending up at Jack's dad-house at mealtime. Yet that's where I found myself tonight, in front of a plate of steak, a pot of plain brown rice, and a bag of raw baby carrots.

APPARENTLY CARROT PARENTS DON'T CARE TO DEFEND THEIR YOUNG...

"I hear your school might stop serving pizza," said Fritz (that's Jack's dad's name). He passed me the bag of carrots.

"Not if we can help it, right Jack?" I said. "Jack, Bee, Danny, and I are fighting for food justice. We made posters, and we're going to try to get other kids to sign our petitions. Our goal is to keep pizza, chicken nuggets, and chocolate milk."

(Quiet chewing for an epic amount of time.)

"We also need to think up a chant in case we have a sit-in," I said. "Or does a chant only go with a march? I can't remember. Anyway, did you come up with any chant ideas, Jack?"

"I can't think of anything that rhymes with pizza."

"Yeah. That's a tough one," I agreed.

(More silent swallowing.)

"So how 'bout those Broncos?" I threw in. "Think they'll make the tournament?" (I don't follow football, but I know Fritz does.)

"The playoffs? Maybe," he said.

"Yeah, possibly," said Jack.

(More quiet chewing followed by clinky plate-clearing.)

After dinner the 3 of us played Farkle, which is this addictive dice game where you shake 6 dice in a plastic cup then roll them onto the table. You'll have to learn the scoring system if you want to play, but it's

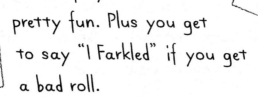

pretty fun. Plus you get to say "I Farkled" if you get a bad roll.

Even Fritz chuckled whenever someone Farkled.

In the morning, we had flapjacks. That's what Fritz calls pancakes. They're beige, so Jack likes them. And if you spread them with peanut butter and top the peanut butter with a drizzle of maple syrup, they're tasty <u>and</u> filling.*

FRITZ'S FANCY 5-STEP FLAPJACK FEAST

1. PUT PANCAKE MIX INTO A BOWL AND ADD WATER.
2. STIR.
3. POUR BATTER ON SKILLET.
4. FLIP.
5. FEED.

p.s. Whenever I go to Jack's dad-house, I wonder what it would be like if <u>my</u> mom and dad ever got divorced. A lot of kids in my class have divorced parents. Jack seems cool with it. But I think I'd miss my dad if I couldn't be with him every day.

CHANT CHOICES

After breakfast, Jack and I tried to write a good chant and discovered it isn't that easy.

Here are our best ideas:

F.E.A.S.T. IS A BEAST!
LIKE THE WITCH OF THE EAST!

SAUSAGE PIZZA, CHOCOLATE MILK!
CHICKEN NUGGETS, _____
(ACK. ALMOST NOTHING RHYMES WITH MILK) :(

WE WANT GOOD FOOD EVERY DAY!
WE WANT PIZZA ON OUR TRAY!

PIZZA, PIZZA, HE'S OUR MAN!
VEGGIES BELONG IN THE GARBAGE CAN!

IF THE MILK'S NOT CHOCOLATE,
THEN YO! WE DON'T WANT IT!

YOU CHOOSE WHAT <u>YOU</u> EAT—SEEDS AND NUTS AND SUCH.
WE'LL PICK OUR OWN LUNCH, THANK YOU VERY MUCH!

Our lunch!
Our choice!
Our school!
Our voice!

P-I-double Z-A.
That spells yumbo any old day!

We like pizza, yes we do.
We like pizza, F.E.A.S.T. won't do!

First you lean to the left,
then you lean to the right.
Then you pick up your pizza and
CHOMP! take a bite.

Which one should we use? Or...maybe you can think of a better one. (Either way, you can e-mail your ideas to aldozelnick@gmail.com.)

WHAT DO WE WANT?

BETTER CHANTS!

WHEN DO WE WANT 'EM?

NOW!

PIZZALESS MONDAY

What you need to understand is that I have eaten sausage pizza for lunch every Monday since I was born. OK, since I started 1st grade at Dana Elementary School. In my world, Monday and pizza go together like, well, Thanksgiving and turkey or Patrick and SpongeBob.

But today when I slid my lunch tray down the line, it wasn't the usual triangular slice of pizza that Mr. Fodder placed on it. Instead, it was something green and blobbish.

"Feast on our new Chicken-Broccoli Fricassee,* Aldo," he said. "It tastes 'sensational'!"

"No pizza?"

"Nope! But you can load up on more veggies at the new salad bar! And don't forget your carton of white skim milk!"

"Gah!"

So during lunch, Jack and Bee and Danny and I went around getting kids to sign our petitions, which was foolproof* timing during the shock of the first Pizzaless Monday. We gathered pages and pages of signatures in 15 minutes.

FREEDOM FROM THIS GLOP?
WHERE DO I SIGN?

Then we skipped our after-lunch recess to take the petitions to Mr. Dobrowski's office.

"Mr. D., you took away my Pizza Monday," I said as I barged in. "Nobody takes away my Pizza Monday. Nobody." I slammed the kids' signatures down on his desk and crossed my arms across my chest.

"Excuse us, Mr. Dobrowski!" Bee said. "What Aldo means is that we've prepared petitions that politely ask you and Mrs. Pooker to reconsider some of the particulars of the F.E.A.S.T. program, which mostly we're in total agreement with."

"A bunch of us kids signed them," added Jack with a ferociousness* in his voice that's not like him. "Even me, 'cause cheese pizza is one of my food groups."

"Good for you!" said Mr. Dobrowki, leaning back in his chair and lacing his fingers behind his head. "I like to see students take some initiative. Mrs. Pooker and I will meet and review your petitions." Then he leaned forward and said a little sharply, "But next time, Zelnick, knock."

"Sure thing, Mr. D!" Bee said as she shepherded us out of his office.

"Whew!" Danny signed.

"You were brazen, Aldo!" said Bee. "Don't you know that you can catch more flies with honey than with vinegar?"

"Pffft," I said, reaching into my backpack for my emergency beef jerky. "Problem solved." And I did that thing where you smack your palms together up and down a few times to show that you've accomplished your task.

Bam! Glad that's taken care of.

SLOW FOOD

Tonight we went with Bee and Mr. Mot on a bike ride to check out the new restaurant.

It's still being finished inside, but Bee gave us a tour. I've never been in a not-open restaurant before! It's like getting to go behind-the-scenes on a movie set or something, only with food. Then we sat in one of the booths and played Farkle and nibbled on figs* Bee filched* from the giant walk-in refrigerator.

Pretty soon Mrs. Goode called us back to the kitchen to taste the fava bean* stew recipe she's experimenting with. "These beans were grown and dried right down the road," she explained. "We're using as many local ingredients as we can."

Mrs. Goode also showed us the bins of white onions, orange squash, and red apples that a Fort Collins farmer had delivered just that morning.

"These beans are colossal!" I said, looking down at the cup of stew she'd handed to me.

YOU GOTTA PROBLEM WITH MY SIZE, CURLY?

"And they're brown—not beige," frowned Jack.

CUZ IN SOUP THIS GOOD, IT'S HARD TO KEEP MY BEANISH FIGURE...

"I have no problem with brown," I said as I chewed a spoonful of stew, "but this needs more salt."

"You know, I think you're right, Aldo," said Mrs. Goode. "Would you like to add some to the kettle?"

So I washed my hands then grabbed an enormous pinch of sparkly salt from a dish sitting on the counter. I stood on a stool and sprinkled it into the giant pot of stew and stirred. I was cooking in a restaurant!

After that we stayed in the kitchen and
helped Mrs. Goode for a while. Mr. Mot chopped
onions and got all weepy about the fabulous French
onion soup he had once in Paris, a long time ago. I
worked some more on my ninja chef skills by rolling
out pastry dough for a fig tart. Bee and Vivi even
made an Arcimboldo face in a bowl!

ARCIMBOLDO CALLED THIS
ONE "THE GARDENER."
CAN YOU TELL WHY?
HINT: TURN YOUR
BOOK UPSIDE-DOWN.

"Cooking from-scratch with real ingredients takes time, huh Aldo?" Mrs. Goode asked me as we pressed the dough into special tart pans with wavy edges. "Do you think it's worth it?"

"I'll let you know after I taste this tart."

She chuckled. "Some people call the way we're doing things here at Fare 'slow food' because it's the opposite of fast food."

"Hey, that's just like the Pilgrims and the first Thanksgiving!" said Bee's sister, Vivi. "They had to make all their own food by hand too!"

(That kid sure knows an awful lot for someone who's only 5.)

I'M A WILD TURKEY, AND IF YOU DON'T LET GO NOW, YOU'LL FIND OUT WHY, PILGRIM.

"Do you have any food that's slow and beige?" asked Jack. "Because I'm famished.*"

So Mrs. Goode made Jack a grilled cheese sandwich with homemade bread and fontina cheese from a local cheese place (she called it a "fromagerie*"). It wasn't exactly what he's used to, but I noticed that he gobbled it up just the same.

And are you wondering about the fig tart? I've always thought the Christmas song that talks about "figgy pudding" was bizarre, because even though I had no idea what it really was, figgy pudding sounded funky.* Well all I can say now is that if figgy pudding is anything like fig tart...then bring me some figgy pudding, and bring it right here!

THE RAPTOR CENTER

After school today, I enthusiastically accompanied by dear mother to the raptor center to help her feed the falcons.

It turned out to be pretty fascinating, because she introduced me to another peregrine falcon—one who's getting better and will soon get released! We didn't get too close though, because Mom said that wild birds have to stay wild.

"We also don't name them because they're not pets," she said. "But to myself I call this one Frightful after the falcon in one of my favorite books. And it's time for Frightful's lunch."

Then mom took me to a room where I could see what happened next on a TV screen. Thanks to a camera in Frightful's room-sized cage, I watched Mom step inside with one alive quail in each hand! She quickly tossed the birds and left the cage.

The quails flew around for just a couple seconds before Frightful swooped down and grabbed one in mid-air. She carried it to her perch and started plucking its feathers. Kinda cool, kinda gross.

I'LL NEVER LOOK AT FANCY LADIES' FINGERNAILS THE SAME WAY AFTER THIS.

Frightful's quail meal made me glad I could simply open a cupboard when I got home and grab a handful of potato chips, which is what I was doing when I heard this weird whirring noise. I followed it upstairs to my parents' bedroom. There was my dad on a walking machine—a machine that wasn't there earlier today.

"I got us a treadmill!" said Dad, who was all red and sweaty in the face. He turned off the machine and let himself slide backwards off the end. "Isn't it fantabulous*! You can walk while you watch TV!"

"Kids don't do treadmills," I said. "They're for old people. No offense."

"Actually, they're for anyone who could use some more exercise. And look—your iPod plugs in right there. Hop on! Give it a try!"

"Nah. I have homework to do."

"OK...well, after your homework then!"

But after my homework I ended up playing 3 hours of Timothy's Final Fantasy Tactics game instead, and I "forgot" all about the dumb treadmill till just now. Aaand...now it's time to go to sleep.

p.s. School lunch today was lentil burgers! That's burgers made out of <u>beans</u> instead of cows! Seriously?! They tasted like mouse poop. Aldo's Army needs to regroup tomorrow for sure.

SIT-IN AROUND

During lunch today (fat-free-whole-wheat lasagna), we decided to give the sit-in thing a try. First we let a bunch of other kids know what we were going to do, so they could join us if they wanted to. (Nobody did.)

Then we sat down in the middle of the cafeteria and locked arms. I noticed right away that in a big room, you don't feel very powerful when you're sitting criss-cross applesauce on the floor.

SOMEHOW I FEEL MORE LIKE A PRISONER THAN A PROTESTER.

I'M ALSO PROTESTING THE FACT THAT DANNY ALWAYS LOOKS SO PUT-TOGETHER. WHAT IS HE, A CUTENESS FACTORY? THAT'S MY JOB!

"Now what do we do?" asked Jack.

"Sit here," I said.

"But we're gonna get in trouble," Bee fretted.*

Most of the kids kept right on eating their lunch and chattering away, paying us no attention, but Mr. Fodder ambled over. "So, you're already fed up* with F.E.A.S.T.?" he said. "But it's only just getting started!"

Danny gave the universal "up to here" sign.

"We demand to speak with Pooker!" I said.

"We do?" said Jack.

"Yes! We turned in our petitions, but the lunches keep getting worse! So now we're taking more drastic action!"

"Good luck with that," said Mr. Fodder. "My beard and I will be in the kitchen." He eyeballed us again then turned and walked away.

"Should we chant?" I asked.

"Um, OK," said Jack. "Let's do the 'Our lunch! Our choice!' one. It sounds the most official."

"I can't do this," said Bee. "Sorry to flake out* on you guys." And she hopped up and blended back in to the sea of kids at the lunch tables.

That left me and Jack and Danny. And since Danny doesn't speak with his mouth, it was just me and Jack who started it:

OUR LUNCH! OUR CHOICE! OUR SCHOOL! OUR VOICE!

Little by little, the chant got us noticed. Clumps of kids grew quiet and listened. A few who understood what we were saying joined in. Then a few more. Then a bunch more. And pretty soon the whole cafeteria was yelling and thumping together to the beat:

OUR LUNCH! OUR CHOICE! OUR SCHOOL! OUR VOICE!

OUR LUNCH! OUR CHOICE! OUR SCHOOL! OUR VOICE!

OUR LUNCH! OUR CHOICE! OUR SCHOOL! OUR VOICE!

OUR LUNCH! OUR CHOICE! OUR SCHOOL! OUR VOICE!

Enter Mr. Dobrowski. He had a panicked, holy-cow look on his face when he careened into the room. But then he put this fingers in his mouth and blew one of those loud, piercing whistles that only a few people can do. That's probably a required skill for principals.

And since we were obviously the ringleaders, he marched over to us.

"So, gentlemen," he said. "What seems to be the problem?"

"We want to talk to Mrs. Pooker. Today," I said. "The F.E.A.S.T. program is a farce.* Did you see today's 'lasagna'?" I tried to air-quote around the word lasagna, but since my arms were linked with Jack's and Danny's, I don't think it had the same effect.

"I don't appreciate this fracas* at all," said Mr. D. "You 3 just earned yourselves after-school detention for a week. Starting today. But if you promise me no more funny business,* I'll see if Mrs. Pooker can come for a meeting."

"But...," I started to say.

"But nothing!" he scolded. "Consider yourselves fortunate* that I'm not suspending you. I'll let you know about the meeting. Now up on your feet, back at your table, mouths closed." And he left.

"So <u>that</u> happened," said Jack, looking a little flustered.*

"Wow," signed Danny.

When I stood up, I felt a little taller. Admiring eyes followed us as we walked back to our table. Yes, I was still hungry, since I only ate one bite of that faux*-sagna, but it was a good kind of hungry. A powerful kind of hungry.

(GRUMBLE)

I DON'T KNOW ABOUT EVERYONE ELSE, BUT I COULD TOTALLY GO FOR SOME FRENCH FRIES RIGHT NOW. I'M <u>POWERFULLY HUNGRY.</u>

MY SIDE OF THE MOUNTAIN

THIS KID LIVES
IN THE ONLY
TREE FORT
I KNOW OF
THAT'S COOLER
THAN OURS.

Turns out detention is no big deal! You just sit in Mr. D's office for an extra hour after school and read! (And you "forget" to tell your parents.)

Remember how my mom mentioned that she calls Frightful Frightful because of the falcon in one of her favorite books? Well I didn't really know what she was talking about until yesterday, when she handed me a beat-up old softcover.

"This is my copy of My Side of the Mountain from when I was a kid," she said. "It's about a boy who raises a peregrine falcon he names Frightful. I think you'll like it."

Sure enough, there on the cover was a falcon that looked a lot like our Frightful, and she was sitting on the boy's shoulders!

"Wouldn't it hurt to have Frightful perched on your neck like that?" I asked.

"Yes. And it wouldn't be safe either. But it makes for an enticing book jacket."

So I started the book today during detention as I nibbled on a bag of fruit snacks. Sam Gribley is the main character's name. He's a teenager, and he runs away from his home in the city to go live by himself in the wilderness. All he has to eat in the story is whatever he can find—or catch—in the forest. I bet he would've liked a fruit snack or 2.

COME BACK, FRUIT SNACK! I'M SO HUNGRY! AND WHY IS WILD BERRY THE ONLY FLAVOR HERE!?

THE GOOSE IS GETTING FAT

In band today we practiced our holiday music. Our band teacher, Mrs. Dulcet, is all in a frenzy* because our Christmas concert is just a few weeks away.

Hey, I just realized that our Christmas concert is just a few weeks away! That means the most blessed season of the year is really and truly upon us! Thanksgiving, with its feasting and turkey and sleeping in and mashed potatoes and stuffing and chillaxing on the couch and days off school and pumpkin pie and rejoicing! Followed by Christmas, with its gifts and more feasting and gifts and days off school...and did I mention gifts?!

So anyway, we were in the middle of practicing the song "Christmas Is Coming" when my pants started really bugging me. It's hard to blow into a trumpet when your pants have shrunk. You have to be able to breathe to be a good brass player!

I sat up straighter in my chair and tried wiggling my derrière a bit to adjust the waistband. Then I planted my lips and blew hard into my horn... and apparently my pants' button couldn't take it anymore. It flew across the band room and hit Mrs. Dulcet square in the forehead.

"Ouch!" she said, raising a hand to her head. "What was that?"

The class giggled while Mrs. Dulcet looked on the floor around her for the cause of her pain. Lucky for me, it was a brown button on brown carpet, and she didn't see it.

THANK GOODNESS FOR WEIRDLY PATTERNED SCHOOL CARPETING.

"Maybe it was a bee," I said. "Or a mosquito!" I nibbled a nail—a nervous habit.

"A bee? In November?" glared Bee, who always knows the truth of every situation.

But Mrs. Dulcet seemed distracted enough by my suggestions that she quit looking and returned to directing our practice. As the minutes ticked by, the red spot on her forehead grew redder and puffier.

At the end of band class, when I stood up to leave, I had to hold the top of my pants together with one hand, then go to the front office to get a safety pin. And after school I snuck into the band room and found my incriminating button.

Whew. Detention may be no big deal, but my parents will freak out* if they find out I'm getting into trouble at school.

FREE AND CLEAR.

WICKED WITCH OF THE F.E.A.S.T.

Jack, Bee, Danny, and I got called out of P.E. (yes!) to Mr. Dobrowski's office today. A black-haired lady sat waiting for us. At first I didn't recognize her because she didn't look like a fish, but then she held out a long, pointy-fingered hand to me and said, "Hello, Aldo. I'm Mrs. Pooker. I understand you and your friends have several grievances about the F.E.A.S.T program."

"Finally!" I said. "This F.E.A.S.T. thing is a total fiasco! Where to begin? Welp, first of all, Mondays are for pizza. There's really no other option, so yeah. Also, chicken nuggets have been making themselves pretty scarce lately, so we're gonna need those back."

Danny's head bobbed in silent but complete agreement with me.

"I'm afraid it's not that simple," said Mrs. Pooker. "I realize the F.E.A.S.T. menu is not perfect yet, but the changes we're making are essential to children's health."

"We completely agree with you," said Bee, trying the honey approach. "Our health is the most important thing, of course. But what's so great is that food that's good for you can taste really good too! For example, my parents are opening a restaurant called Fare—"

"That's very nice, my pretty," Mrs. Pooker interrupted. She was looking witchier and witchier with every syllable that bubbled from her mouth. "But schools operate under constraints more challenging than those of some trendy new restaurant."

Bee pressed her lips together tight and raised one eyebrow at Pooker then. I've been on the receiving end of that furious expression of Bee's before. It's not pleasant. But Pooker didn't seem to notice. I snuck a piece of gum into my mouth and started chewing.

"What about you other children?" She turned to look at Jack.

"Well, all I wanted to tell you is that cheese pizza is one of my 4 food groups," said Jack softly.

"Pizza is hardly a food group. You'd stop being so finicky if you got hungry enough. Over time, you'll learn to appreciate chicken-broccoli Mondays."

Bee swallowed her fury and tried her chirrupy voice one more time. "But pizza with wheat crust and healthy toppings—including cheese— really is good for you! And delicious!"

STRANGE. THIS FLY DOESN'T SEEM TO CARE ABOUT HONEY AT ALL...

"And chocolate milk...," I added. "That's basically a children's right. I think it might even be in the Constitution or one of those inalienable documents."

"Pizza is a junk-food fad* that needs to fade. And chocolate milk and sugary soda are among the main causes of childhood obesity." Puker had the nerve to look pointedly at my stomach as she said this.

"So you're saying we're being force-fed* F.E.A.S.T. whether we like it or not?" I was flabbergasted.*

"I'm saying that it is the responsibility of adults to ensure the children in their care are healthy. But I do thank you for sharing your thoughts." Then she climbed on her broom, cackled wickedly, and flew away.

SHE DIDN'T REALLY FLY OFF ON A BROOM, BUT THAT'S SURE WHAT IT FELT LIKE.

So that's how <u>that</u> went. I'm sitting on my bed, fuming.* Now what?

ARCIMB-ALDO

Today in art class we put the finishing touches on our Arcimboldo-style self-portraits. Mine came together quite awesomely, I must say. I even found a place for a doughnut. And bacon. And pizza! Take THAT, Mrs. Puker.

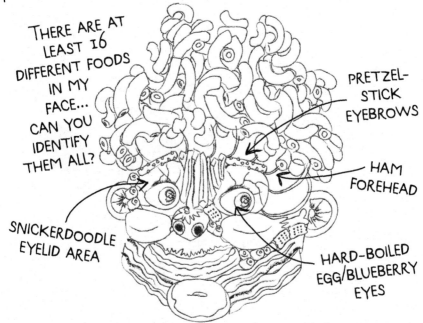

THERE ARE AT LEAST 16 DIFFERENT FOODS IN MY FACE... CAN YOU IDENTIFY THEM ALL?

PRETZEL-STICK EYEBROWS

HAM FOREHEAD

SNICKERDOODLE EYELID AREA

HARD-BOILED EGG/BLUEBERRY EYES

I think I'll find a picture of a gold frame somewhere on the internet, print it out, and put my Arcimb-Aldo inside of it. Then I'm gonna ask my mom to make a color copy of the whole thing to stick on the front cover of this sketchbook. Right after I finish this bag of fish crackers.

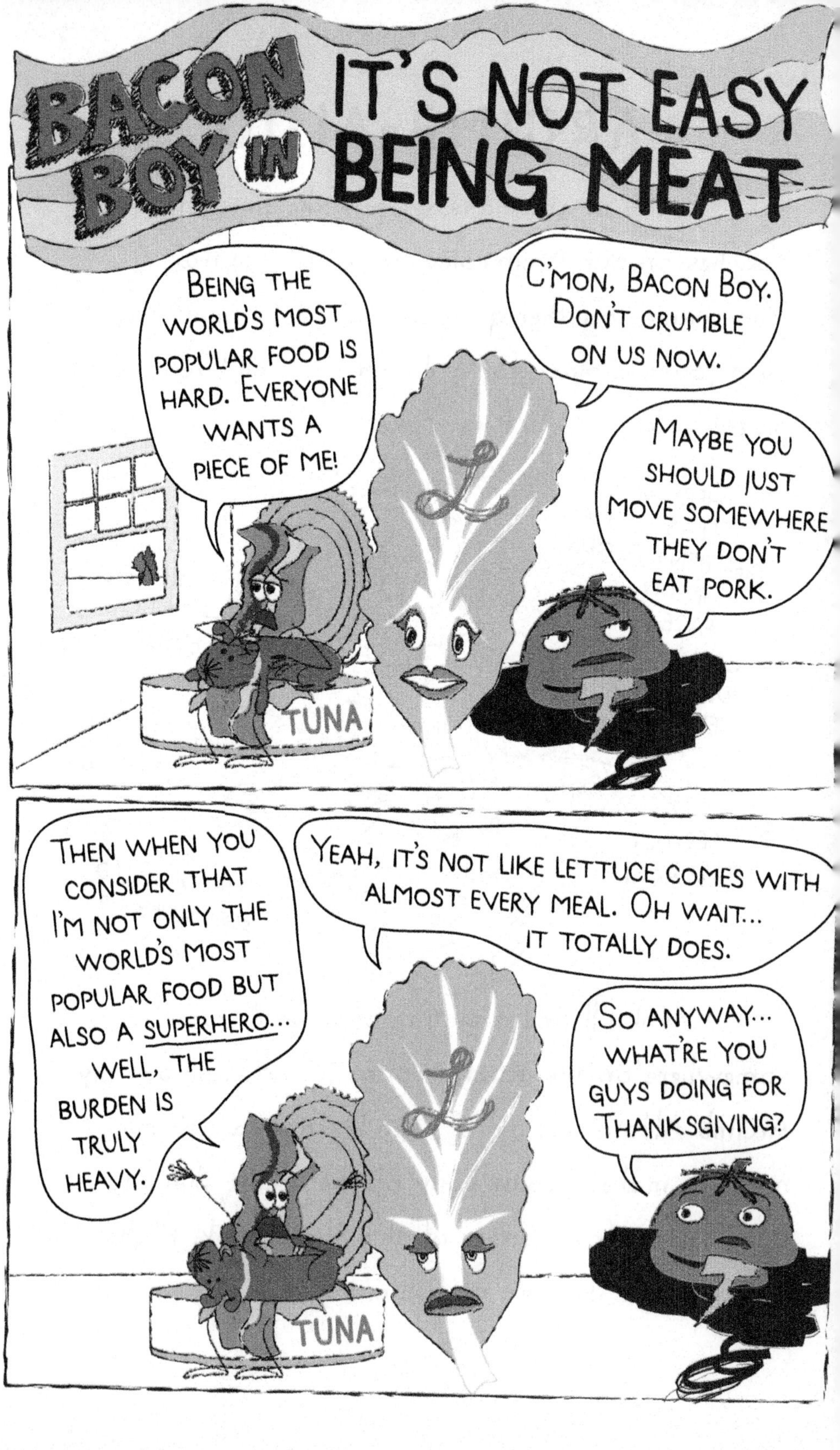
BACON BOY IN IT'S NOT EASY BEING MEAT
BEING THE WORLD'S MOST POPULAR FOOD IS HARD. EVERYONE WANTS A PIECE OF ME!
C'MON, BACON BOY. DON'T CRUMBLE ON US NOW.
MAYBE YOU SHOULD JUST MOVE SOMEWHERE THEY DON'T EAT PORK.
TUNA
THEN WHEN YOU CONSIDER THAT I'M NOT ONLY THE WORLD'S MOST POPULAR FOOD BUT ALSO A SUPERHERO... WELL, THE BURDEN IS TRULY HEAVY.
YEAH, IT'S NOT LIKE LETTUCE COMES WITH ALMOST EVERY MEAL. OH WAIT... IT TOTALLY DOES.
SO ANYWAY... WHAT'RE YOU GUYS DOING FOR THANKSGIVING?
TUNA

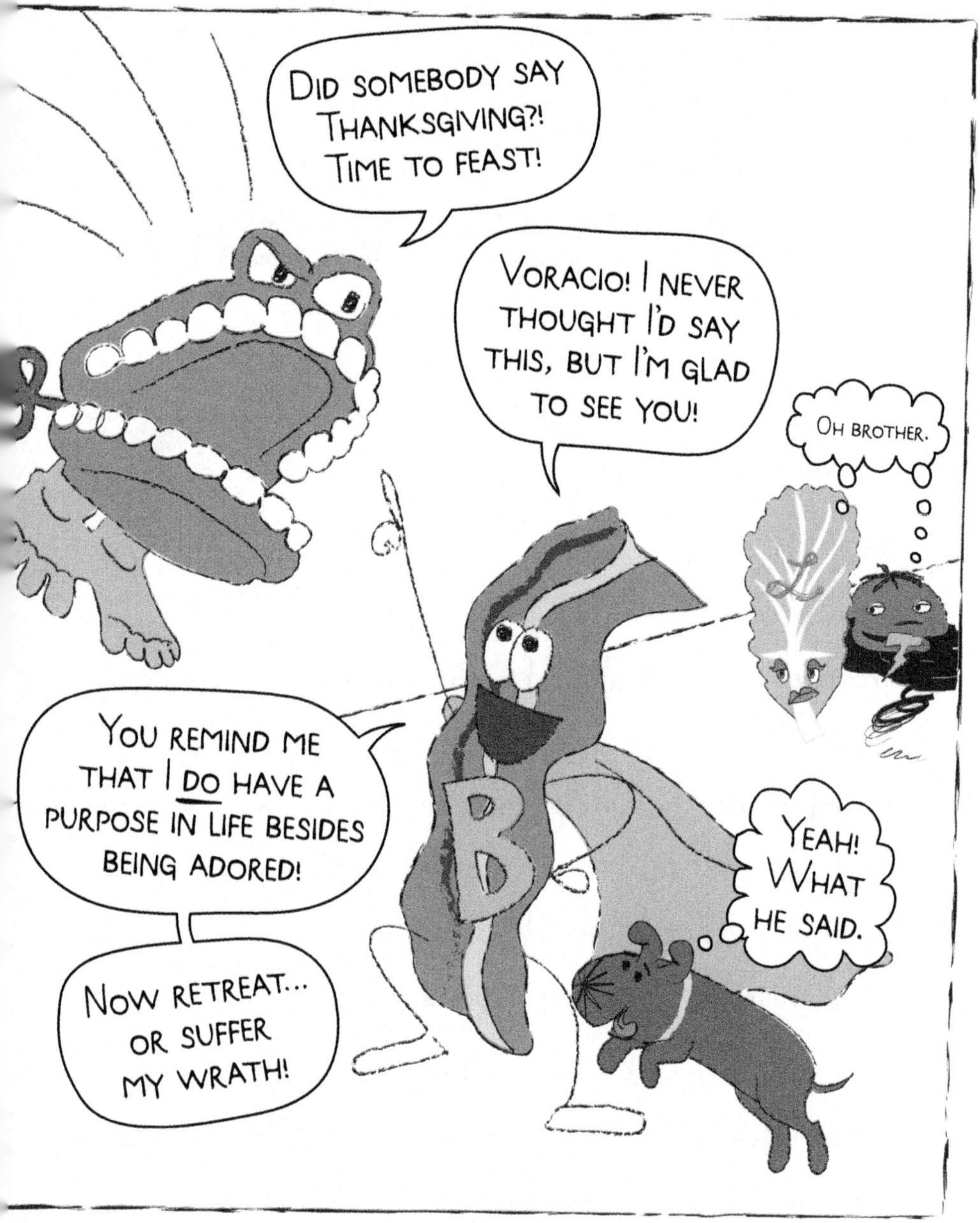
DID SOMEBODY SAY THANKSGIVING?! TIME TO FEAST!
VORACIO! I NEVER THOUGHT I'D SAY THIS, BUT I'M GLAD TO SEE YOU!
OH BROTHER.
YOU REMIND ME THAT I DO HAVE A PURPOSE IN LIFE BESIDES BEING ADORED!
NOW RETREAT... OR SUFFER MY WRATH!
YEAH! WHAT HE SAID.

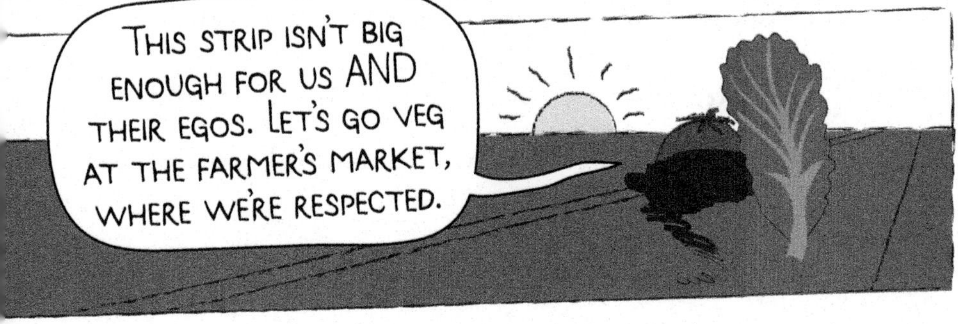
THIS STRIP ISN'T BIG ENOUGH FOR US AND THEIR EGOS. LET'S GO VEG AT THE FARMER'S MARKET, WHERE WE'RE RESPECTED.

ABUELO'S WISH

Today I tried to forget my school-lunch troubles for a while. After detention I went with Jack and his mom to visit Abuelo (that's Jack's grandpa) at the place where he lives now. It's called Fountain House, but it's not really a house. It's more like a special hotel for old people who can't live by themselves anymore because they forgot how.

Abuelo and I got to be *amigos* last month when I saved his life on Halloween night. (Not like it's a big deal or anything.) He was sitting in his recliner chair when we walked into his room.

"*Hola, Abuelo,*" said Jack. "*Te traje una piedra nueva.*" (That means, "I brought you a new rock.")

Jack gives Abuelo a rock every time he visits. He set the new one alongside the row of others on top of Abuelo's dresser.

"Hola, Abuelo," I said. "Me llamo Aldo." (That means, "My name's Aldo." I wanted to remind him because he can never remember it.) Then I also said, "Soy el niño mapache." ("I'm the raccoon boy." You'll have to read Egghead to understand that one.)

Abuelo just smiled his enigmatic smile at us.

"Let's take Abuelo down to the cafeteria, boys," said Mrs. Lopez. "I bet he'd like some company for dinner tonight."

So the 4 of us ambled down a long hallway with nature photos of animals like foxes and ferrets hanging on the walls. I guess it's like bringing a little of the outdoors indoors for people who don't get out anymore. As we walked, Mrs. Lopez said hello to all the other feeble* old people who live there. They seemed so delighted just to see us, especially me and Jack.

The food was pretty beige, so Jack loved it— noodles with butter, plain chicken breast, and dinner rolls. I noticed that Abuelo ate just a couple bites, though. Maybe he wasn't hungry tonight.

In the middle of the cafeteria splashed a giant fountain—the kind where you can throw in a coin and make a wish. After we'd eaten, Mrs. Lopez gave us a handful of pennies, and Jack and I took turns flipping them in, seeing who could land one on the highest level. Pretty soon all the old people gathered around us. They laughed as we tossed the pennies from harder and harder positions—sitting on the floor, closing our eyes, etcetera. We mostly missed and had to chase down the pennies as they bounced and rolled across the hard floor.

Finally Abuelo shuffled over and plucked a penny from my palm. He turned around, and with his back to the fountain, flipped it over his head and straight into the top level. *Bam.* Just like that. Everyone clapped and whistled and cheered, and Abuelo smiled and bowed before quietly making his way back to his room.

I wonder what he wished for?

FIRED-UP FRIDAY

THIS IS HOW I FEEL WHEN I'M FIRED UP: FEARSOME, UN-SHOWERED AND WEARING WAR PAINT, LIKE IN THAT *BRAVE* MOVIE. (ONLY WITHOUT THE KILT.)

Last night after the visit to Abuelo's, Bee, Danny, Jack, and I had an emergency fort meeting to talk about what to do next about F.E.A.S.T. We'd tried posters, petitions, a sit-in, and even a meeting with Mrs. Pooker, but so far nothing had worked!

Even Bee was fired up because Mrs. Pooker had treated us like children.

So we made a plan. This morning, we got to school early and handed out a sign to any kid who didn't say no. We made a bunch of them last night in the fort using regular white paper and paint-stirrer sticks my dad had in the garage.

We held up our signs and walked around in a circle chanting, "Our lunch, our choice! Our school, our voice!" Yup, we were picketing Dana Elementary School.

OUR LUNCH!
OUR CHOICE!
OUR SCHOOL!
OUR VOICE!

OUR LUNCH!
OUR CHOICE!
OUR SCHOOL!
OUR VOICE!

OUR LUNCH!
OUR CHOICE!
OUR SCHOOL!
OUR VOICE!

OUR LUNCH!
OUR CHOICE!
OUR SCHOOL!
OUR VOICE!

When the bell rang, most of the kids handed us back their signs and scurried inside, but we didn't stop. We kept right on marching. Of course, that brought Mr. Dobrowski out to talk to us.

"You need to go into your classroom now," he said.

"This is more important than book learning," I said. "This is like...the Boston Tea Party. Only for pizza."

"I'll have to call your parents," he warned.

"But Mrs. Pooker didn't even listen to us!" said Bee. "This is the only way to make our voices heard!"

"How about if we do it only during lunch hour and after school?" said Jack.

"Hm. I guess that's fair," said Mr. D. "But my patience is growing exceedingly thin. No more disruptions inside the school or during regular class time, all right?"

So we gave up our Fish Friday lunch to picket some more (not a big sacrifice, and besides, I packed a fluffernutter*), and then after school, when we picked up our signs again, guess who was there waiting for us? A reporter and a photographer from the local newspaper! They asked us questions and took our picture. They said we'd probably be in Sunday's paper!

Woot! We're gonna be famous! And now maybe the weight of public opinion will come down on Mrs. Pooker and she'll melt to our demands!

FLASH DANCE

HELLO MY BABY,
HELLO MY HONEY,
HELLO MY
RAGTIME GAL...

Instead of sleeping in: dance class again this morning. Gah.

It's becoming a Saturday morning routine now...Goosy blows into our sleepy house like a tornado of happiness, carries off me and my dad in her spin, and drops all 3 of us onto the wooden floor of the dance studio, where we all face a giant mirror and watch ourselves try to copy the teacher's lightning-fast movements and stay in beat with the music.

It's as exhausting as it sounds, believe me.

My dad is totally into it, though. In between daily walks on the treadmill, he's been practicing The Frug at home every chance he gets. And today he and Goosy talked to the other dance class students about doing a flash mob* performance sometime soon.

"You mean we'd do The Frug in public somewhere? Like the mall?" I asked.

"Sure!" said Goosy. "That would be a blast!"

"We Zelnicks were blessed with natural rhythm, and we really should share it," said Dad.

"I am flexible," I admitted. "But I'm pretty sure rhythm skipped my generation. So I'll pass on the flash dance thing. Who's up for frozen yogurt on the way home?"

Anyway... now I can kinda do one weird dance. I'm sure that will be an impressive addition to my résumé:

ALDO ZELNICK'S RÉSUMÉ

- MOSTLY GOOD GRADES.
- EXPERIENCED GAMER.
- FLEXIBLE (PHYSICALLY—NOT SOCIALLY OR DAILY-ROUTINE-WISE).
- FLOATS WELL IN SWIMMING POOL.
- EXCELLENT EATER.
- TALENTED DRAWER.
- KNOWS A LITTLE SIGN LANGUAGE. AND ESPAÑOL.
- LIFE RESCUER. (NO BIG DEAL)
- REPEATEDLY FAILS FITNESS TESTING BUT CAN DANCE THE FRUG.

THE SUNDAY PAPER

Thank goodness my parents still get the newspaper—I mean the actual printed kind that's magically delivered to your front porch during the middle of the night—because, well, for one, the color Sunday comics (Goosy calls them the "funnies") are still pretty darned awesome, even if you can find a lot of good comics online, and also because...

This morning, there I was on page 4! I read the article in between bites of frittata.*

HUNGER GAMES
DANA STUDENTS PROTEST SCHOOL LUNCH CHANGES

The article below the photo talked about how Mrs. Pooker's F.E.A.S.T. program is being tested at Dana Elementary and how all us kids hate it. The reporter quoted me as saying that removing pizza from the menu is like "making baseball and apple pie illegal in the Unites States of America." <u>Nice.</u>

(Perhaps that was a bit of a stretch, but the way I figure it, you can't go wrong appealing to people's patriotic-ness.)

Even Mr. Fodder was mentioned in the story. He told the reporter that the kids aren't eating many of the new recipes and that the food is going to waste. Good one!

If this news story doesn't put pizza back on our plates tomorrow, I don't know what will.

MY HERO!

IF ABSENCE REALLY DOES MAKE THE HEART GROW FONDER, I MIGHT NOT BE PREPARED FOR HOW AWESOME TOMORROW'S PIZZA WILL TASTE.

JUST ANOTHER FRANTIC* MONDAY

Not only was today's lunch <u>not</u> pizza, it was a whole new level of abominableness: tofu surprise. Well let me tell you, it was no surprise to me that the lunchroom trashcans were filling up faster than Mr. Fodder could dump them. They looked like tofu volcanoes.

Just a sec. I hear my dad calling me from downstairs. He's asking if I want to play FOX, which I do not. BRB.

Sometimes in life, you go to play a harmless game of FOX (which you didn't even want to play) and *bam*, your whole world shatters. I thought life was supposed to be fun and good and happy—full of my favorite things—but it's not. It's just <u>not</u>.

Here's what happened: When I got downstairs, Dad convinced me to play basketball. Ever since we had that chat about helping each other be active, he's been Mr. Fitness—treadmilling and shootin' hoops and dancing up a storm.

So there we were, playing FOX in the driveway. Pretty soon Timothy and Mom joined in. Timothy was doing trick shots, so Dad tried to get fancy too. He got a running start and dribbled toward the hoop. Then he launched himself into the air, his body silhouetted against the dusky November sky. A one-handed slam?! Incredible!

"Wow!" I said

"OWWW!" screamed Dad.

And he clutched his chest. And he crumpled to the ground.

After that is a noisy blur. Dad was moaning but trying to get up, even though his face was crunched in pain and he couldn't get up, and Mom was yelling at him to lie still, and Timothy was saying he learned CPR in P.E. and laying his head on Dad's chest, and Mom was flipping open her cell phone and punching numbers, and before I could even inhale, sirens were blaring toward our house, and Jack's dad was jumping from a firetruck like a superhero in a red helmet, and then an ambulance was zooming in too, and paramedics were swarming my dad—MY DAD!—and strapping a breathing mask to his face and laying him on a tray and lifting him into the back of the ambulance, and I was grabbing onto him like if I couldn't keep a hold, my heart would stop beating, and Mom was telling me no, I had to stay with her, but I was saying (and I might have been yelling) that Dad and I went together no matter what, no matter what, and then I was holding his huge hand in the ambulance and he was smiling at me from under that plastic mask, and then we were rushing into the emergency doors at the hospital just like on TV, and doctors and nurses were chattering all around us, and I had to let go of Dad's hand because they were rolling him away...and his hand waved to me then dropped palm-down flat on the cart.

My heart hurts just retelling that part.

Then Mom and Timothy rushed in. The doctor told us that Dad needed some tests. They took us to a room where we put our arms around each other and waited.

Finally, finally, the doctor came back. Her lips turned up at the corners and she said, "Mr. Zelnick is going to be fine. All the initial tests show that his heart is OK. We think he tore a muscle in his chest, which can be very painful. But just to be sure, we'd like him to stay here at the hospital overnight so we can keep an eye on him."

That's when my mom cried, and 1 or 20 drops might have come from my eyes too, and Timothy high-fived me, and we got to go see my dad, who was sitting up now and breathing with no mask, and there was some group hugging and love yous. Then Jack's dad came in, and we all talked about what happened. And what (thankyouthankyou) didn't.

By then it was late. Mom said we needed to go home and let Dad rest.

"See you tomorrow, sport," Dad said as he gave me a one-armed hug. (It hurts his chest when he uses his right arm.) "Don't worry...I'm fine. I think my dunking days might be over, though."

He seemed fine. But I'm still kinda worried. I'm home in my bedroom writing this. I feel fidgety* and sleepy and worried and happy, all at the same time.

FOOD FIGHT!!!

Grrr. Mom is making me go to school today, even though it's the Tuesday before Thanksgiving and the rest of the week is a holiday. I said I'm grouchy and tired, and since Dad's still at the hospital, staying home from school is obviously the best plan. But she said she just talked to the doctor on the phone. Dad's fine and she's going to bring him home this morning. So yeah. I gotta go.

I definitely should have skipped school.

But instead I walked there with Jack, as usual. In Ms. Munroe's class we had an art show where we talked about our Arcimboldoish self-portraits and hung them in the hallway. Mine was one of the best for sure, and even though I was kinda frazzled,* I felt glad that my dad was OK and Thanksgiving was almost here. So far so good.

Then grammar and language arts, ho-hum, then—ack—P.E....and the dreaded 1-mile timed run.

The mile was the last activity in our fitness testing unit. I can't actually <u>run</u> a whole mile, ever, but today I <u>really</u> wasn't up for it. So while the other kids ran circles around me, I <u>walked</u> the mile. And as I walked, I got furiouser and furiouser about this fitness testing and BMI thing and recording everyone's numbers—because even if you're trying, like my Dad, you can still be hurt and your family can still get really scared. And then I thought about F.E.A.S.T. and how uber unfair that is. So by the time I'd finished my 17-minute mile, I'd worked myself up into quite a frenzy.

Which...was bad timing, because lunch came next. And instead of the usual before-Thanksgiving hot lunch of creamy chicken potpie in a flaky crust, Mr. Fodder spooned puke-green slime onto my tray.

"Spinach stroganoff," he said. "Happy holiday."

I carried my tray to the table where my friends and I always sit. I noticed they weren't putting any food in their mouths. So I looked around, and all I saw were kids chattering and laughing—but not eating. (Except the lucky ones who brought sack lunch today.)

So I set down my tray then climbed to stand on top of our table. I cupped my hands around my mouth.

"Attention, Dana Dingoes! Attention! Attention!" I was yelling, but it was hard to get everyone to listen in a noisy cafeteria. I tried again. "My fellow Dingoes, we cannot tolerate this abuse to our digestive systems any longer! I will keep fighting F.E.A.S.T. until all our favorite foods have been restored!"

"Get down, Aldo!" Bee tugged at my pants. "You're gonna get in trouble!"

"Yes, harsh punishment may come down upon me because I am speaking out," I continued, "but I will not be silenced!" Then I bent down to pick up my tray, which was my biggest mistake.

"This 'food,'" I said, air-quoting as best as I could while holding a lunch tray, "is not edible. Have any of you actually enjoyed even one bite of this lunch?" By now most of the kids were listening, yet not one raised a hand. I balanced a blob of the spinach goop on my fork and raised it into the air. "Healthy food that no one eats is <u>not healthy</u>!" My raised arm jerked back and forth as I emphasized. "We must throw away F.E.A.S.T. and START OVER!" And I kid you not, as I said the word "throw," the spinach accidentally flew off my fork and hit Fiona, one table over, smack in the ear.

MY SPEECH JUST KINDA GOT AWAY FROM ME. AS DID MY SPINACH.

"Food fight!" someone yelled.

"Wait a second!" I screamed, but it was too late. Spinach and brown noodles and apple slices were flying every which way. It was like being in the middle of a food tornado. I climbed down from the table and sat, putting my head down and waiting for what I knew would come next. It was time to face the music.*

"SSSSSSS!" Just as I thought, it was Mr. Dobrowski's earsplitting whistle. I looked up. Food stopped flying, and every kid turned to look at <u>me</u>.

"Zelnick!" he barked. "You stay here. Everyone else, back to your classrooms!" The room emptied. "You're suspended," Mr. D said to me. "Effective immediately. Stay here until someone comes for you." And he stomped away, shaking his head.

Mr. Fodder sat down across from me. "I saw what happened," he sighed. An apple slice clung to his beard net. "Why didn't you tell him that you weren't the one who started the food fight?"

"Because it was my fault. Partly, at least, even though I didn't mean for it to happen."

Goosy picked me up and brought me home. I'm gonna leave out the whole getting-bawled-out-by-my-parents scene, because you can probably imagine it. (Think of the worst mad-parents moment you've ever experienced and multiply it times infinity.) But after I got a chance to say I was sorry and tell my side of the story, Mom and Dad calmed down a little and there was more hugging and love yous.

"Enough talk," said Goosy. "Time for action. That cafeteria isn't going to clean itself."

So while Dad stayed home to rest, the rest of us went back to Dana Elementary to clean things up and make things right. When we got there, Mr. Fodder was already mopping. Somebody (I suspect Goosy) must have called our friends, too, because Bee and her family and Jack and his parents and Danny and his mom and Mr. Mot showed up to pitch in.

"What <u>was</u> this crud anyway?" asked Bee's mom as she scraped up a spinach splat.

"I don't understand why cafeteria food should taste bad or boring," Jack's mom agreed. "Poor kids. And poor Abuelo! He's eating in a cafeteria every day now too."

For once, food talk didn't make me hungry—it made me come up with a brilliant plan! So when we were done scrubbing, I rounded everyone up to thank them for helping clean up the giant mess I'd made—and to ask them for one more giant favor.

GIVING THANKS

THIS IS IT! THIS IS MY BIG SCENE!

THANKSGIVING DAY!

I've never been so fatigued* after a Thanksgiving feast as I am at this moment. I mean sure, after feeding on a lovely plateful of turkey with mashed potatoes and gravy, you always get sleepy, but I am tiiired. I guess it's because I spent the entire day working instead of my usual turkey-day couch-potatoing.

But it was my idea, so I guess I won't complain. Much. ☺

By 7 o'clock this morning, my family and I were in the kitchen at Fountain House (that's Abuelo's old-people hotel, remember?) cooking alongside Bee's family and the Fountain House food staff. We seasoned and stuffed 10 raw turkeys and got them into the ovens, then we started peeling potatoes (white and sweet), roasting beets and Brussels sprouts, cooking cranberries, and rolling pie dough. Mr. Mot mixed up a colossal batch of his famous cranberry-orange chutney, and Bee tossed a Jolly Green Giant-sized salad. And Bee's parents brought a lot of colorful fruits and vegetables from their new restaurant, which they whipped up into weird-but-surprisingly-good-tasting side dishes. Oh, and bread! The Goodes kneaded dough into crusty, delicious homemade bread too.

Mrs. Lopez and Abuelo rolled tamales in corn husks. "It's what he wished for," I told her as I walked by with a stack of plates. She gave me a "what are you talking about?" look, but I knew I was right because Abuelo nodded and winked at me.

Goosy recruited Vivi, Jack, and Danny to help her make decorations. By the time the feast was ready, the Fountain House cafeteria looked quite festive. My dad and Jack's dad sat together at a greeter's table and gave everyone a nametag.

Timothy helped the Fountain House old folks through the buffet line first. I've never seen so many smiling seniors. Next came the guests. I personally waited on Mrs. Pooker and Mr. Dobrowski and their families. (Yup, we invited them, and they came!) I figured I owed them that. Even Mr. Fodder showed up. Without his hairnets and wearing a jacket and bow tie, he looked almost fashionable.*

DID SOMEONE SAY HOMEMADE GRAVY?

Finally I got to load up my own plate. I sat next to Jack, who'd already finished eating.

"I tried the cranberries," he said.

"No way! They're red! That's just about as non-beige as food can get! Did you like 'em?"

He shrugged. "I'm still alive."

And for entertainment? The disco dance students—including yours truly—held a Frug flash mob between the main course and dessert. Dad directed us. Good thing I hadn't already sampled the pumpkin, pecan, and cherry pies or I would have burst another button for sure.

Before they left, Mrs. Pooker and Mr. Dobrowski flagged me down. They said they'd enjoyed the Thanksgiving dinner very much and that Bee's parents had offered to help improve the F.E.A.S.T. menu.

"So you're not a witch after all?" I wanted to say but didn't. Instead I said, "Great! And how long am I suspended? Do I get to stay home until after New Year's?"

HAVE YOU CONSIDERED A CAREER IN POLITICS?

Mr. D laughed. "Actually, I talked with your parents too, and we agreed that having you help Mr. Fodder in the school cafeteria over your lunch hour for a month would provide you with a better learning opportunity than suspension. So congratulations. You're a junior lunch man."

Sigh. At least I won't need a beard net.

FAREWELL

My dad put his good arm around my shoulder as we watched Frightful's release at the county open space today. She spread her wings and glided across the sky like defying gravity is no biggie.

"That was some Thanksgiving you made happen yesterday, Aldo," Dad said.

"Yeah. I've never seen that many mashed potatoes! It was like a dream come true."

"You know, I'm thankful I have a son who takes responsibility for his actions and makes things right."

I leaned a little into his sweater. I felt thankful for lots of things but didn't say. Instead, I listened to his heartbeat: *lub-dub, lub-dub.*

Mom walked over to us. "Oh I just love watching falcons fly," she gushed. "We should celebrate! Lunch at Fare on the way home?"

"Nah," I said. "Maybe tomorrow. I'm still full from Thanksgiving! Let's follow this trail for a little bit. We can see where Frightful goes."

"Leo, Aldo just said he wanted to walk!"

"I'm standing right here, Mom. Sheesh." And I started stepping down that path, which I'd never been on before.

"F" GALLERY

Mr. Mot used to be an English teacher. He's a word nerd, and he likes to help me use awesome words in my sketchbooks. I mark the best words with one of these: * (it's called an asterisk). When you see an * you'll know you can look here, in the Gallery, to see what the word means. If you don't know how to say some of the words, just ask Mr. Mot. Or someone you know who's like Mr. Mot. Or go to aldozelnick.com, and we'll say them for you.

fabulous (pg. 43): awesome; wonderful

face the music (pg. 131): take responsibility for something bad you did

fad (pg. 106): something that's popular but just for a little while

famine (pg. 7): when there's hardly any of that food to be found

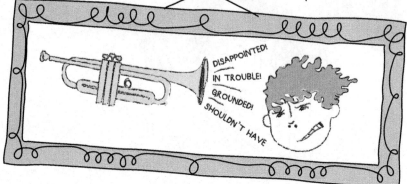

DISAPPOINTED!
IN TROUBLE!
GROUNDED!
SHOULDN'T HAVE

famished (pg. 87): so hungry you could eat your own foot. Not really... but still, SUPER hungry.

fanatic (pg. 34): someone who's not just a fan of something—they're an uber fan

fantabulous (pg. 90): fantastically fabulous

fantastic (pg. 21): so awesome it seems like it couldn't possibly be real

farce (pg. 95): ridiculously dumb

HM. MAYBE A LITTLE HOT SAUCE...

Fare (pg. 17): the name of the Goode's restaurant but also, when it's not capitalized, a word that means "food"

fashionable (pg. 136): stylish according to today's fads

fastidious (pg. 71): super neat and clean

fated (pg. 70): what you're born to do, whether you like it or not

fatigued (pg. 134): really tired

fattoush (pg. 60): salad mixed with chunks of pita bread and a lemony-garlicky dressing.

Actually sounds kinda good. Might need to give it another try.

IF THE CAFETERIA DISH HAD LOOKED LIKE THIS, I WOULDN'T HAVE HAD TO MAKE SUCH A FUSS.

faux (pg. 96): pronounced just like "foe" but means fake

> I MAY BE FAKE, BUT THE FEROCIOUSNESS IS REAL.

fava bean (pg. 83): one of the big, burly uncles in the peanut/lentil/lima family

fed up (pg. 93): so annoyed over and over again by something you can't escape that you're starting to freak out

feebish (pg. 42): a word I invented that means boredom hunger

feeble (pg. 112): really weak and breakable-looking

fell swoop (pg. 24): together at the same time

fend (pg. 32): sticking up for or taking care of

ferocious-ness (pg. 81): snarly, attacking anger

festive (pg. 19): in a happy, partyish mood

fiasco (pg. 62): a total disaster

fictitious (pg. 40): made-up; pretend

fiddlesticks (pg. 13): a nice-girl-like-Bee expression that means "darn it!"

> YOU FLEAS BIT MY DOG. PREPARE TO DIE.

fidgety (pg. 126): so hyper you wiggle parts of your body

fierce (pg. 53): way cool (but also ferocious)

figs (pg. 83): a weird fruit

Fig Newton (pg. 52): a fig-filled cookie shaped like a mini-Hot Pocket with the ends cut off

filched (pg. 83): stole something little

filet mignon (pg. 30): the best kind of steak ever invented

filibuster (pg. 133): stand up in front of everyone and make a really long speech (usually to stall for time)

filling (pg. 75): food that makes your stomach feel full and happy

finagle (pg. 72): to make something happen the way you want it to

fine-feathered friend (pg. 27): a good buddy

finicky (pg. 8 and other places): super-picky about something, such as what you'll eat and won't eat

Fireball, Atomic (pg. 23): super-hot cinnamon candies

fired up (pg. 17): really excited

fit-for-a-king (pg. 15): the best of the best

flabbergasted (pg. 106): super-surprised by something because even though it makes no sense, it's happening

flair (pg. 64): a stylish way of doing something

flake out (pg. 94): quit; chicken out

flash mob (pg. 118): a surprise group dance in a public place

flatter (pg. 57): say nice things to someone, even though you might be exaggerating

flatulence (pg. 72): a more scientific way of saying "farting"

THAT WALTER DOG IS A MINOR LEAGUER.

flawless (pg. 11): perfect, like my plan to get more Christmas gifts this year than ever. Mwah-ha-ha...

flee (pg. 26): run away. (By the way, "flea" with an A is the dog-biting bug kind.)

fleetingly (pg. 70): there for just a tiny bit of time and then it's gone

floundering (pg. 23): doing something awkwardly—in this case, walking

fluffernutter (pg. 117): a peanut butter-and-marshmallow-creme sandwich

fluke (pg. 66): a weird coincidence

fluorescent (pg. 11): a kind of lightbulb that uses less energy

flurries (pg. 14): just a few snowflakes here and there; the snow equivalent of rain sprinkles

flustered (pg. 96): anxiously bothered

flying the coop (pg. 44): running away and not coming back

folderol (pg. 133): nonsense

food chain (pg. 71): living creatures that need each other for food, like falcons eat sparrows eat caterpillars eat plants

foodie (pg. 72): someone who loves and appreciates good food

foolproof (pg. 79): can't possibly fail

foot, my (pg. 38): an expression that means "That's a bunch of nonsense!"

footprint, carbon (pg. 14): how much carbon dioxide you add to the air when you do something that uses a fossil fuel*

for the birds (pg. 53): throw-it-in-the-trashcan bad

force-fed (pg. 106): made to accept something even though you don't want to

foreboding (pg. 38): worry that something bad is going to happen

fortunate (pg. 96): lucky

145

fossil fuel (see footprint, carbon): energy that lives under the ground, like oil, that somehow took millions of years to be made from dead plants and dinosaurs and other living things getting smooshed together

fracas (pg. 95): noisy troublemaking

fragrance (pg. 15): smell

frame of mind (pg. 13): how you're feeling and thinking at the moment

frantic (pg. 122): rushed with excitement or worry; frenzied

frazzled (pg. 127): worn out from too much hectic activity

freak out (pg. 101): have a complete meltdown

freaky (pg. 58): creepy weird

frenzy (pg. 99): worked up about something in a good way or in a bad way

fretted (pg. 92): worried out loud

fricassee (pg. 78): a fancy word for a stewish mixture

frittata (pg. 120): a big omelettish thing baked in the oven

fritter, apple (pg. 68): a fried doughnut with cinnamon-sugar apples cooked into it. What's not to love?

IN A FROUFROU FRAME OF MIND

146

fromagerie (pg. 87): a cheese-making company

Frug, The (pg. 70 and other places): sounds like "froog." A dance you can look up on YouTube if you want to see what it looks like.

froufrou (pg. 60): fancy and frilly

fuddy-duddy (pg. 69): someone who's afraid to try new things

fuming (pg. 106): so angry it feels like smoke is coming out your ears

fungus (pg. 61): the mushroom, mold, and mildew category of things that grow. Mmm! (Not.)

funky (pg. 87): weird and possibly icky

funny business (pg. 96): tricky or troublemaking behavior

furnishings (pg. 15): stuff that makes an empty space a room

further ado (pg. 21): more blah-blah-blah

furtively (pg. 23): sneakily, because you hope no one sees you do it

SHHH. IT'S BETTER WITH CHOCOLATE!

fury (pg. 41): Atomic Fireball-like anger

futile (pg. 113): something that is just not possible, so you might as well not even try it

MY NEIGHBORHOOD

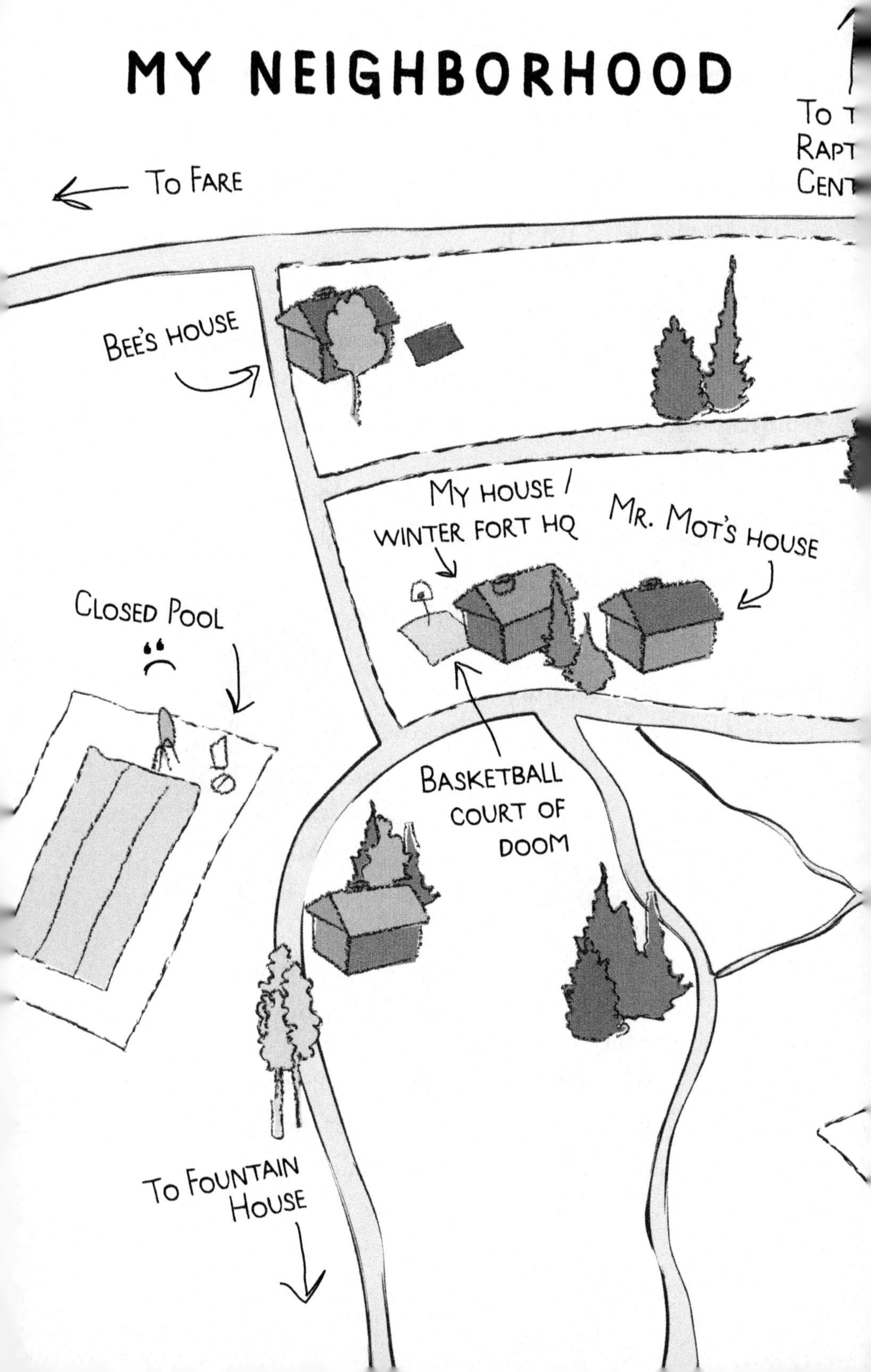
To T
Rapt
Cent
To Fare
Bee's house
My house / winter fort HQ
Mr. Mot's house
Closed Pool
Basketball court of doom
To Fountain House

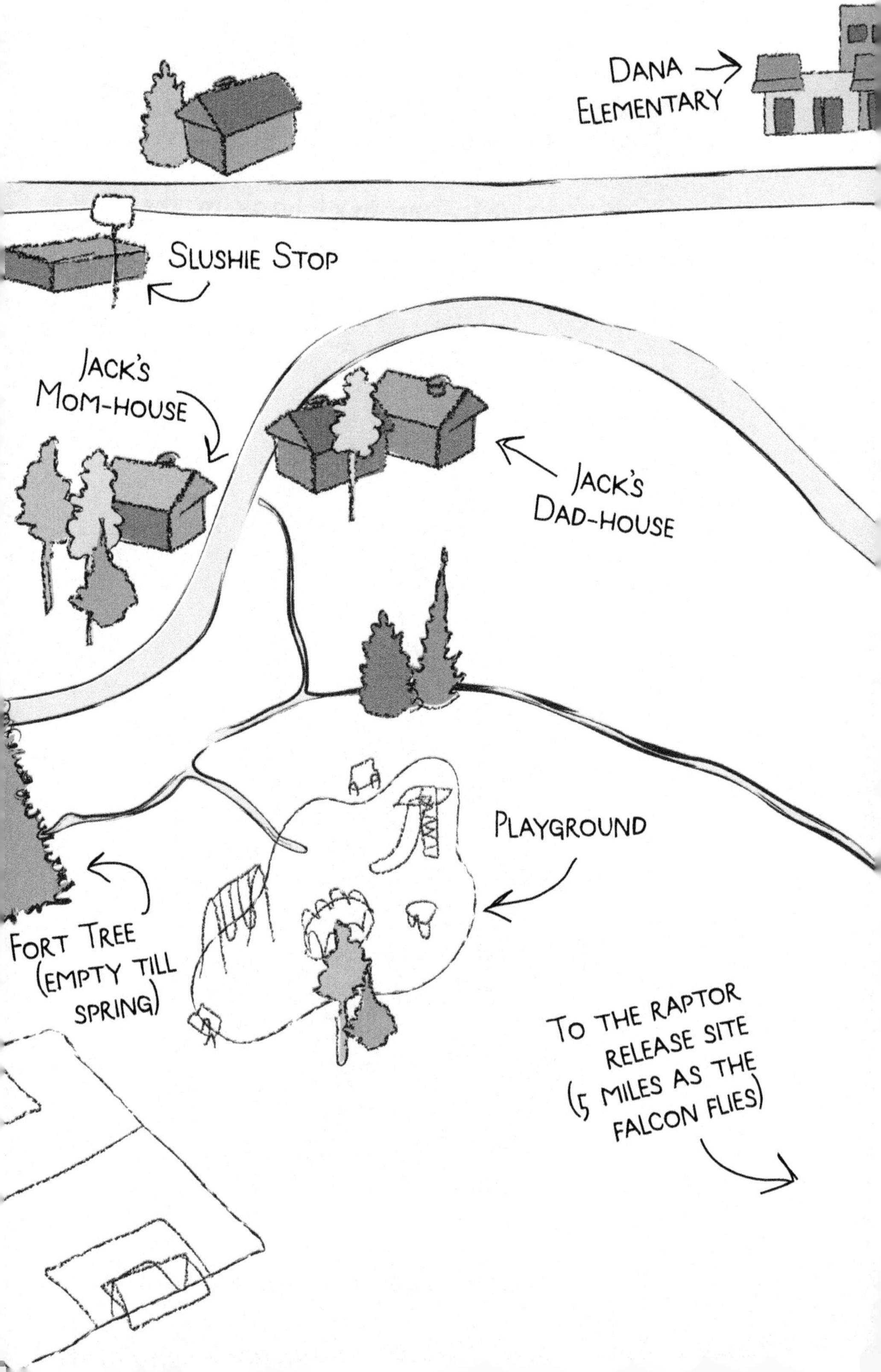
DANA ELEMENTARY
SLUSHIE STOP
JACK'S MOM-HOUSE
JACK'S DAD-HOUSE
PLAYGROUND
FORT TREE (EMPTY TILL SPRING)
TO THE RAPTOR RELEASE SITE (5 MILES AS THE FALCON FLIES)

Sneak a Peek!

Dive right into the next book in the audacious Aldo Zelnick Series here.

AN EXCERPT FROM **GLITCH**, BOOK 7 IN THE ALDO ZELNICK SERIES!

CHRISTMAS COUNTDOWN

Guess what my mom just handed me?! No, not the usual Saturday afternoon pile of clean laundry. It's my chocolate Christmas calendar!

EVERY DAY UNTIL CHRISTMAS, YOU GET TO OPEN A LITTLE PAPER DOOR WITH A NUMBER ON IT. BEHIND EACH DOOR IS AN ITTY-BITTY PIECE OF CHOCOLATE IN A DIFFERENT SHAPE. IT'S A CALENDAR AND

Yesss. That means today's December 1st... and <u>that</u> means just 24 more days till P to the R to the E to the S to the E to the N to the T to the S! PRESENTS!

Mom also said it's time for me to start making my list! Every year my brother Timothy and I write lists of the Christmas presents we're hoping for, and we tack them on the kitchen bulletin board.

AN EXCERPT FROM *GLITCH*, BOOK 7 IN THE ALDO ZELNICK SERIES!

Then *bam!*, a bunch of the things appear gift-wrapped and gorgeous* under the tree on Christmas morning. All in all, not a bad system.

And...now Mom's yelling up the stairs to me, saying I need to go bring in the mail from our mailbox at the end of the driveway. Sheesh. Can't a kid have a little yuletide planning time? BRB.

OK, somebody has been holding out on me all these years. How come I never knew about this fancy Christmas catalog? It came in today's

CHRISTMAS

THE GUMBALL PINBALL MACHINE

mail, and it's got the most fantastic toys and gizmos* I have <u>ever</u> <u>seen</u>. I mean, I would've put <u>lots</u> of this stuff on my Christmas lists before—if I'd only known it existed!

AN EXCERPT FROM *GLITCH*, BOOK 7 IN THE ALDO ZELNICK SERIES!

Take the **Inflatable Backyard Log Flume**, for example. Who doesn't want one of these?

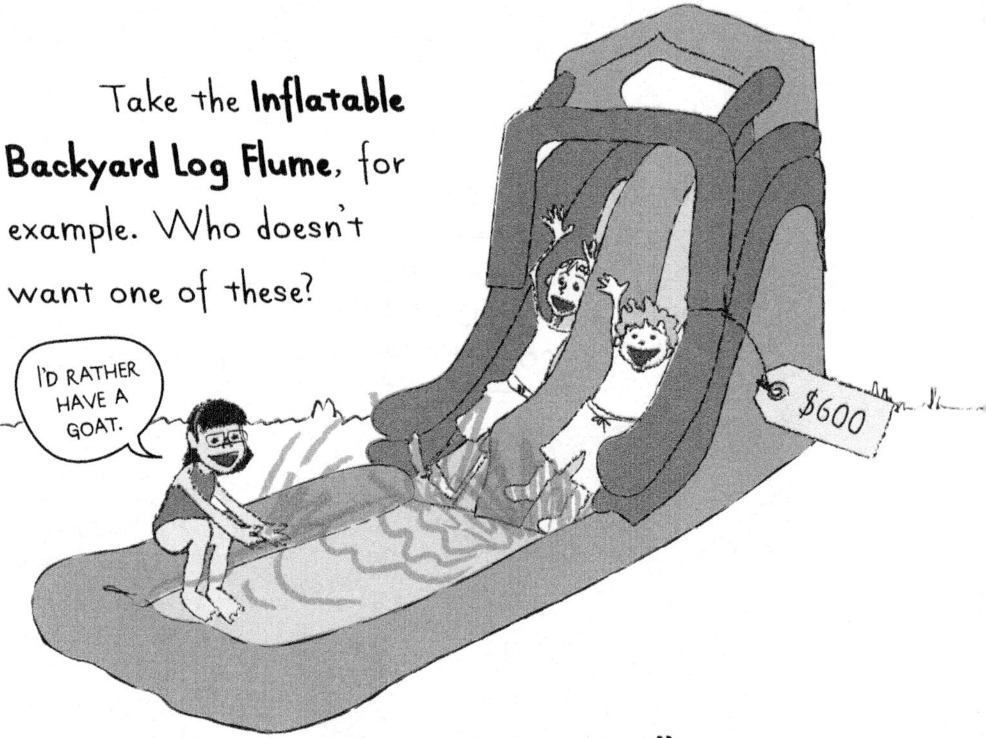

I'D RATHER HAVE A GOAT.
$600

Or the **All-Terrain Electric Transporter**! It's like an uber scooter you don't have to scoot yourself!

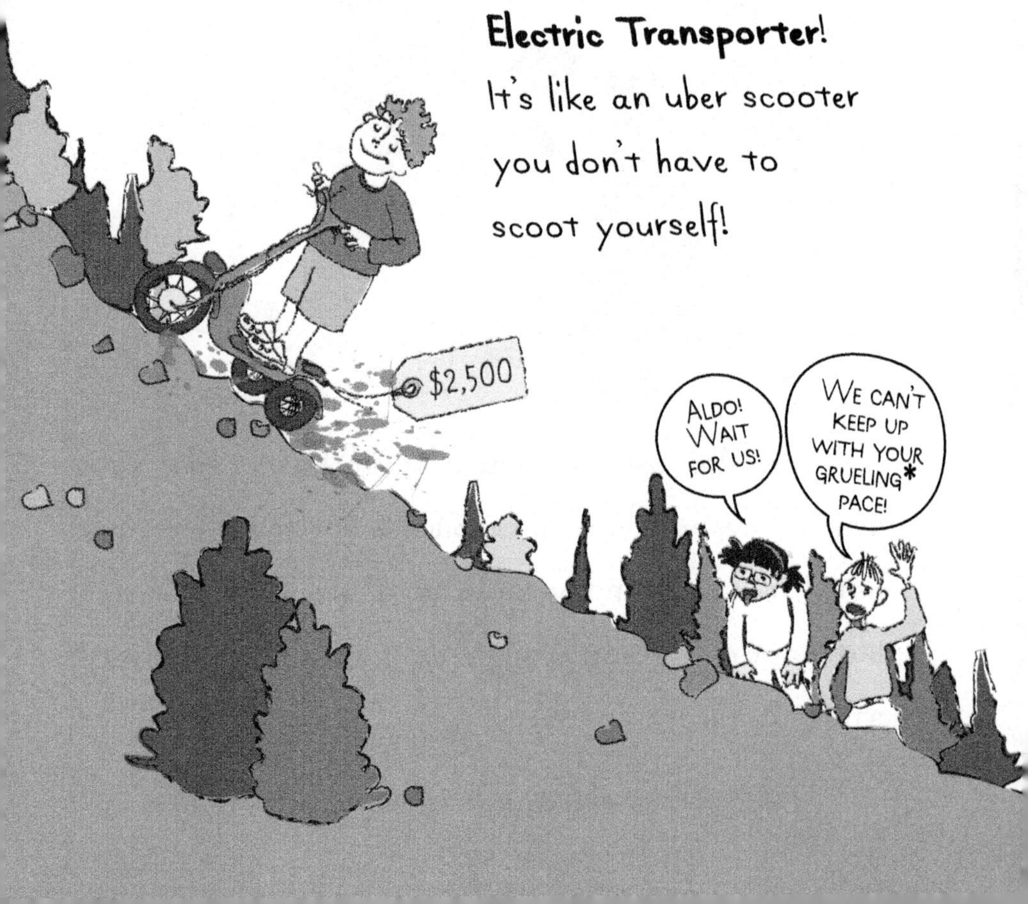

$2,500
ALDO! WAIT FOR US!
WE CAN'T KEEP UP WITH YOUR GRUELING* PACE!

Or holy brain-freeze...
the Classic Snow-Cone Cart!

Welp, this magical catalog has opened up a whole new world of possibilities for my Christmas list. I mean, I don't wanna be a greedy* McSneedy, but apparently somebody's getting all this groovy* stuff. So why not me?

AN EXCERPT FROM *GLITCH*, BOOK 7 IN THE ALDO ZELNICK SERIES!

OH BROTHER, WHY ART THOU?

Whatever you do, don't have an older brother.

Maybe an older sister's OK...I'll never know, 'cuz God only seems to make boy Zelnicks...but an older brother is basically a torture device th smells like Gillette Power Rush deodoran

Today was Timothy's 15th was all, "This is <u>my</u> day, bro having granola* and (He just made but he ac

ACK!
WHAT HAPPENS NEXT?
Get your hands on the full
book at aldozelnick.com
or your local bookstore or library.

ABOUT THE *award-winning* ALDO ZELNICK COMIC NOVEL SERIES

The Aldo Zelnick comic novels are an alphabetical series for middle-grade readers aged 7-13. Rabid and reluctant readers alike enjoy the intelligent humor and drawings as well as the action-packed stories. They've been called vitamin-fortified *Wimpy Kids*.

Part comic romps, part mysteries, and part sesquipedalian-fests

(ask Mr. Mot), they're beloved by parents, teachers, and librarians as much as kids.

Artsy-Fartsy introduces ten-year-old Aldo, the star and narrator of the entire series, who lives with his family in Colorado. He's not athletic like his older brother, he's not a rock hound like his best friend, but he does like bacon. And when his artist grandmother, Goosy, gives him a sketchbook to "record all his artsy-fartsy ideas" during summer vacation, it turns out Aldo is a pretty good cartoonist.

In addition to an engaging cartoon story, each book in the series includes an illustrated glossary of fun and challenging words used throughout the book, such as *absurd, abominable*, and *audacious* in *Artsy-Fartsy* and *brazen, behemoth*, and *boisterous* in *Bogus*.

BAILIWICK PRESS

www.bailiwickpress.com | www.aldozelnick.com

ALSO IN THE ALDO ZELNICK COMIC NOVEL SERIES

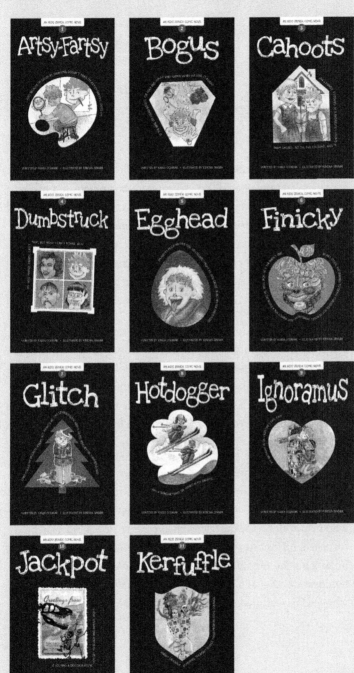

ACKNOWLEDGMENTS

"I come from a family where gravy
is considered a beverage."

— Erma Bombeck

Like Aldo, we come from food-centric families, where the day's activities can (and often do) center around the lusciousness of a just-picked tomato, the succulence of a perfectly grilled steak, or the divinity of a favorite sauce. Our finicky main squeezes, on the other hand, have more in common with Jack; they've been known to leave the room when the conversation turns to cuisine and meal planning, especially at holiday times, and the food worship gets too pentecostal.

Giuseppe Arcimboldo provided the perfect entrée into a storyline that lives at the crossroads of the art of food and the food of art. If you're not familiar with his 16th-century paintings, we urge you to look them up on Wikipaintings.org or ogle them up close in one of the many world-class museums that house them, as Karla did in Vienna a number of years ago. Whether you find them fascinating or frightful, they're certainly remarkable.

For this Thanksgiving book, we'd like to share our gratitude for Renée, who good-naturedly fosters order in our office; Judy Scherpelz of Fort Collins' Rocky Mountain Raptor Program, who helped fine-tune the falcon chapters; the Slow Sanders, who furnish abundant story fixes; and Launie, whose design finesse is unfailingly the very finest. Finally, we give thanks for our fabulous families—foodies and non-foodies alike—and for Aldo's Angels, who feed us with that most sustaining of fare—faith in our work.

ABOUT THE AUTHOR

Photo by Amy Fesenmaier

Karla Oceanak has been a voracious reader her whole life and a writer and editor for more than twenty years. She has also ghostwritten numerous self-help books. Karla loves doing school visits and speaking to groups about children's literacy. She lives with her husband, Scott, their three boys, and a cat named Puck in a house strewn with Legos, ping-pong balls, Pokémon cards, video games, books, and dirty socks in Fort Collins, Colorado.

ABOUT THE ILLUSTRATOR

Kendra Spanjer divides her time between being "a writer who illustrates" and "an illustrator who writes." She decided to cultivate her artistic side after discovering that the best part of chemistry class was entertaining her peers (and her professor) with "The Daily Chem Book" comic. Since then, her diverse body of work has appeared in a number of group and solo art shows, book covers, marketing materials, fundraising events, and public places. When she invents spare time for herself to fill, Kendra enjoys skiing, cycling, exploring, discovering new music, watching trains go by, decorating cakes with her sister, making faces in the mirror, and playing with her dog, Puck.

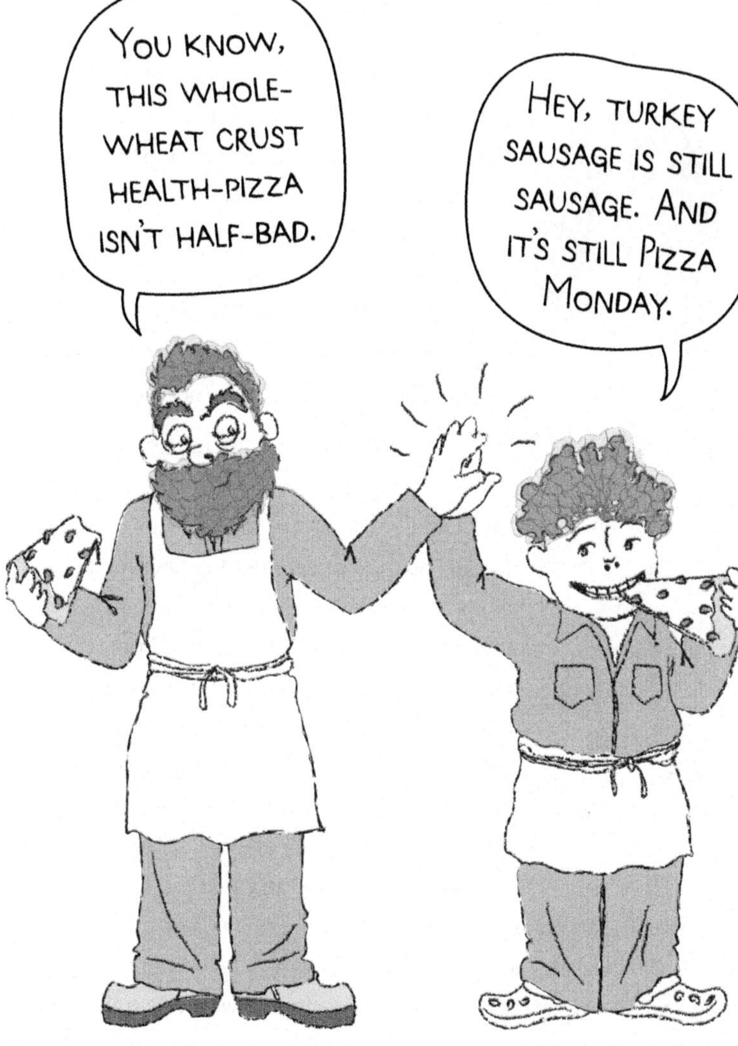
YOU KNOW, THIS WHOLE-WHEAT CRUST HEALTH-PIZZA ISN'T HALF-BAD.
HEY, TURKEY SAUSAGE IS STILL SAUSAGE. AND IT'S STILL PIZZA MONDAY.

CPSIA information can be obtained
at www.ICGtesting.com
Printed in the USA
LVOW03s1456081217
559113LV00005B/10/P